DREAMS OF MOLLY

LORI BEASLEY BRADLEY

❦ I ❦

S herri Lambert woke from another frightful dream about the blonde in the beaded, blue dress. She pushed the blankets back, sat up, and rubbed at her gritty eyes. The morning sun filtered through the lace curtains of her bedroom window. They moved with the soft breeze that carried the scent of honeysuckle from the nearby hedgerow.

Sherri heard a rooster crow from the farm down the road and twisted her head toward the open window. She sighed and ran her fingers through her tangled red curls.

Time to get my lazy ass up, I suppose. If I don't get those last chapters finished, my publisher is gonna be sending a hit team for me.

Sherri, who wrote romance novels using the penname Whiskey Treat, had a few final touches to polish her latest installment of her Western Trilogy about a schoolmarm and her romantic adventures in the Old West.

She'd written her first novel in the series four years earlier and had been lucky enough to snag an aggressive agent who signed the book with a major Romance Publisher in New York.

Sherri preferred writing Historical Fiction without the sappy romance angle, but the agent had talked her into tweaking her original story into a Happily-Ever-After Romance and it had won some awards. The agent had secured a lucrative contract for Sherri and chosen a juicier pen name. Sherri Lambert sounded too tame for an author of Erotic Romances, her agent had insisted.

Whiskey Treat had been born. Sherri thought it was a cheesy pen name but went along with her agent's urging. She'd learned early on that arguing with agents and editors was an act of utter futility.

Whiskey Treat's main female characters tended to be pretty, petite blondes who wore bright blue. That was because for as long as Sherri could remember, she'd been having dreams about a pretty, blue-eyed blonde in a bright-blue beaded dress. The girl's dress wasn't from the western era, but Sherri adjusted.

Sherri could close her eyes and see the girl as if she was an old friend or close relative. Sherri had no idea who the girl was and thought she might be a figment of her imagination brought about by old movies she watched with her grandmother, because the girl had a striking resemblance to the actress Carol Lombard.

Sherri swung her long, bare legs off the bed and dropped her feet onto the stiff pile carpet of the bedroom floor. She could still remember when her grandparents had the carpet installed back in the mid-seventies while Sherri was still attending Barrett Consolidated High School. The harvest-gold pile had faded to a duller shade and was pilled, with years of wear and dust from their little farm. Granny had been so thrilled to get that carpet. Sherri could still remember the woman's broad smile as she arranged her furniture. The carpet was old now and stiff beneath her feet.

I'm not gonna miss this carpet either. I hope the wood floors are still in good shape.

Emmett and Brenda Lambert had been killed in a car accident the year before while on a Sunday afternoon drive into town to visit the Dairy Queen. They'd topped a hill on the country blacktop and run into a combine stalled in the middle of the road.

The county coroner had told Sherri the couple in their eighties had probably been killed instantly and not suffered. She'd closed her eyes many times and imagined her grandfather slamming on the brakes of his old Ford sedan and her grandmother bracing her hands on the dash and screaming as they rushed toward the big green piece of farm machinery.

Sherri knew they'd suffered, if only for a few minutes of sheer, agonizing terror. They'd been found in the wreckage holding one another's hands.

After the agonizing funeral, Sherri had flown back to Palm Springs, made arrangements with a real estate agent to sell her condo, packed up her things, and driven a Penske truck stuffed with her furniture and personal belongings back to take up residence in the old, single-story farmhouse where she'd spent so many happy summers as a child and during her teenage years.

She and her parents had lived in a suburb of Chicago. Sherri had spent her school breaks with her father's parents on the farm just outside Barrett. After her parents divorced, when Sherri was twelve, she'd moved to the little farm permanently and eventually attended high school in Barrett.

Having spent her first several years attending large suburban schools, it had been difficult for Sherri to adjust to the smaller rural school. In

Wheaton, she'd studied in an advanced placement program for gifted students.

In the smaller school outside Barrett, her academic achievements earned Sherri ridicule from the other students, and she'd spent a lot of time weeping in the bathroom after being called a teacher's pet or smart-ass *Chicago* girl.

Her grandparents hadn't understood her depression or her 'acting out', as they'd called it, when she got into high school. She'd experimented with sex, drugs, and alcohol.

It was the seventies, for god's sake. Everybody was doing it. It was the 'don't knock it 'til you've tried it' generation and I thought I had to try it all.

High school had been a struggle for Sherri socially. She never felt like she fit in with any group. She was a smart kid, but the smart kids weren't cool, and Sherri had wanted desperately to be one of the cool kids. She had friends in that group, but not close friends.

Sherri lived in the country and had graduated from a rural elementary school. She wanted to be accepted by the townies in Barret, but she never was. Most of the Snot Squad, the upper-crust town kids, had made her life hell.

One of her first novels had been a cathartic retelling of those horrible days. She'd set the story in a small Colorado town named Hope and had called the novel *Lost Hope*.

It had been one of those things a writer does to work through her past. *Lost Hope* had been a catharsis and the fumbling beginning of Sherri's career as an author.

The book had been self-published and had sold a few copies. It wasn't until Sherri had changed her pen name to Whiskey Treat and republished the book, using that name, that it began to sell. Bookstores added her self-published books to their shelves and sales of *Lost Hope* picked up.

Stop wallowing in the past, Lambert, and get your ass up. You have work to do or there won't be any more books on the shelves.

Sherri trudged into the kitchen and started the Mr. Coffee. She'd seen the advertisements for those nifty, one-cup machines on late-late night television, but Sherri preferred making a full pot and refilling her cup from that, rather than buying those expensive little plastic cups and using one every time she wanted another cup of coffee in the morning or while she wrote.

She stared around the dated kitchen and sighed.

This place needs a make-over worse than I do.

On the round, oak table was a stack of catalogues and home decorating magazines Sherri had leafed through and folded down the corners of pages with things that interested her for the renovation of the old house.

After moving into the old farmhouse, Sherri had been stuffing some things into the closet and happened to notice a loose piece of paneling. When she peeked behind it, she'd found, to her utter amazement, a rough, log wall. Curious, Sherri had rushed outside and pulled off a few pieces of the brown, shingle siding and found more stacked logs chinked with a mortar of some sort. The old farmhouse had originally been a log cabin.

Sherri had thought back but couldn't remember her grandparents ever telling her much about the house or even when they'd initially moved into it. She knew her father had been born in it and that was in the late thirties, but she thought they'd moved here from Oklahoma before the Great Depression and the devastation of the Dustbowl in that state.

Her grandparents had always been very evasive about the past and after being shut down several times, Sherri had simply stopped asking about the house and family history.

Maybe we have outlaws or gangster in our past they didn't want to admit to. Maybe there were cattle rustlers or members of The James Gang or the Lambert family. I need to do one of those Ancestry searches to find out. Who knows, there might just be a book in there somewhere.

Making a trip into Barrett to do some research on the property was on Sherri's to-do list for the not too distant future. She'd made up her mind to gut the old house and take it back to its original log cabin state.

An appointment with a company specializing in the historical renovation of cabins had been scheduled, and Sherri looked forward to a visit from one of their representatives tomorrow. She had the catalogues and magazines handy to show him her ideas.

While she waited for the coffee to brew, Sherri went into the dated bathroom to relieve herself. She glanced at the pink, porcelain fixtures and the matching four-inch square tiles on the wall with the row of black accent tiles along the top and grimaced.

I'm sure as hell gonna be glad to see this shit gone. I don't care if the I Love Lucy retro thing is all the rage today. I hate it.

Sherri turned on the shower and shrugged out of her terry robe. As steam rose to the yellowed Celotex tiles on the ceiling, she sighed with memories of her beloved grandparents. Both her grandparents had been heavy smokers and all the ceilings retained the yellowed remnants of decades of cigarette smoke.

Sherri brushed a tear from her cheek and

stepped into the tub. She luxuriated under the hot spray, squirted some shampoo onto her hair, and worked it into a lather. There were few simpler pleasures than a hot shower in the morning. She rinsed the shampoo from her hair and applied some coconut-scented cream rinse. After rinsing out the conditioner, Sherri attended to her body with a soapy washcloth.

As she washed her face, she felt a tender spot on her cheek and frowned, remembering her dream from the night before.

Her pretty blonde had been arguing with someone. It had been the same illusive man, but Sherri never had a clear picture of his face—she never did.

She remembered his angry, dark eyes as he yelled at the blonde girl and drew back his massive fist. Sherri remembered the fist and she recalled rough fingers around her—the girl's throat. He'd been choking her—the blonde--and he'd hit her on the same cheek that was now tender on Sherri's face. She brought up her hand to touch the tender, lightly throbbing spot on her face and frowned. This had never happened in one of her dreams before.

Sherri turned off the water, stepped out of the tub, and reached for a towel. She patted the water from her body and then wrapped her head in the thick, soft towel. Sherri reached for her robe and slipped her arms back into it.

With her damp hand, Sherri wiped the condensation from the mirror of the chrome medicine cabinet and peered at her reflection in the wet glass.

To her amazement, she saw a blue bruise on her cheek, and she probed it gently with her fingers. As she stared at her reflection, Sherri adjusted the front of her robe and gasped at purple splotches around her throat. They looked like finger marks.

What the hell?

Sherri studied her reflection closer in the streaked mirror. She prodded the spots gingerly and gasped at how tender they were to the lightest touch.

Now, how in hell did I manage that? She touched her aching cheek. *Now, that, I guess I might have done sleeping with my ring pressed into my cheek, but how the hell did I manage fingerprints on my throat? I'm sure I didn't choke my-self in my sleep.*

Sherri stood staring into the mirror, and she narrowed her eyes into a squint as her vision began to blur. Her face became distorted in the wet mirror and another face became superimposed over hers.

Bright blonde hair cut into a short, curly bob replaced her longer red hair, while large, round, blue eyes stared back at Sherri rather than her green ones.

This is too weird. I feel like I'm in the middle of a bad Sci-Fi flick.

"Don't get flustered, Doll," the blonde said, "it'll fade in a day or two and you can cover it easy enough with a touch of pancake if you have it."

A sudden dizziness overcame Sherri as she whipped her wet head around to look for the person speaking. The bathroom was empty except for her and the reflection of the blonde in the foggy mirror.

Sherri eased down onto the pink toilet before she passed out and took the chance of seriously injuring herself on the heavy ceramic fixtures in the cramped, old bathroom. Sherri's heart pounded in her chest as she put her head between her knees and stared at the tiny hexagon-shaped pink and black tiles on the floor.

I swear it's all this damned pink. I may throw up just from that alone. I can't believe Granny put this shit in here or that Paw-Paw let her.

Yes, she could. Her grandmother had been a

woman of her times and singularly attentive to her grandfather's wants and needs. He had never denied his devoted wife anything she'd wanted.

Sherri thought her grandparents' relationship was one most women only dreamed of. The aged couple had been married sixty-seven years when the accident had taken them, and they rested beside one another now in the local Baptist Cemetery.

Her parents' marriage had only lasted thirteen years. Sherri had been married three times, but none had lasted, and she had no children. Sherri often thought her parents' endless screaming and fighting about her father's many affairs had left a bad taste in her mouth for marriage and Happily-Ever-Afters.

She couldn't, for the life of her, figure out how she could write them. There was a lot to be said for a good imagination.

Her parents did keep in touch. Her mother had remarried, moved to Georgia, and had three more children. Sherri knew them, but not well. They exchanged Christmas Cards and saw each other's posts on Facebook. Her father had remained in the Chicago area, married, and divorced again. She'd seen him at her grandparents' funeral and at the reading of the will where Sherri had been bequeathed the property.

"This place should have come to me," her father had protested. "What does she need with it? She lives in California and could care less about the dump."

"And you live in Chicago," Sherri had said with tears brimming in her eyes. "Paw-Paw wanted me to have it."

Her father had turned on her with the rage in his eyes she'd seen as a child when he'd turned on her mother. "But you don't need it," he'd yelled, "and I do. I can sell the damned place to one of those stupid farmers down here for a pretty penny. I have other children to think of, you know. I'd like to have something to leave *them*."

Yah, right. You want the money to spend on one of your bimbos. You don't care about your other kids any more than you ever cared about me.

"It's mine and I'm moving into it," Sherri had growled, making her decision to leave Palm Springs then and there.

She hadn't spoken to her seventy-year-old father since and probably never would again. He'd filed a lawsuit to contest the will, but it had never seen a courtroom.

Let one of your other kids worry about burying you, Dad.

Sherri took deep breaths and squeezed her eyes shut against the sudden wave of nausea. She caught a whiff of coffee and decided that was what she needed and maybe a toasted bagel. Her supper the night before had been a cup of yogurt and a can of peaches. Maybe that's why she'd had bad dreams and choked herself in her sleep.

I seriously need to think about a better diet.

Sherri trudged into the kitchen, took down a mug she'd stolen from a Waffle House in Texas and poured some hot, black coffee from the pot. She set the mug onto the table and popped an everything bagel into the toaster. Soon the savory onion aroma of the bagel joined that of the coffee and Sherri went to the stainless steel, side-by-side refrigerator and took out the butter dish.

❦ 2 ❦

As Sherri sat and buttered her hot bagel, her cell phone chimed with a text message. She wiped her hands on her robe and went into the living room to grab the phone lit up on the coffee table. She opened it to find a text from Realistic Renovations.

RR: Our technician finds himself available this early afternoon for your consultation. Is it convenient for you to move up your appointment?

SL: Of course, I'll be home all day today. Just let me know when to expect him.

RR: He will arrive at your location between twelve-thirty and one. Thank you for any inconvenience this schedule change may have caused.

After her second cup of coffee and her bagel, Sherri did a quick tidy up of the house. She made her bed, rinsed up her dirty dishes, and threw a load of clothes into the washer. Then she pulled on a pair of jeans and a turtleneck sweater. She dabbed a little concealer over the bruise on her face and grimaced.

I still can't imagine what I could have done in my sleep to have caused that, but I look like I've been in a damned bar fight.

At eleven-thirty Sherri opened her laptop and checked her email.

As she'd been dreading, there was a short note from her editor at the publishing house, wondering when she could expect the next and final manuscript of her series. They wanted to get it into rotation for the upcoming holiday season.

She also noted that she had been in contact with Sherri's agent about what to expect next. Was she thinking about another series? Would it be historical or contemporary?

Well, it's good to know they want more. I guess I'd better get to work and finish this one.

Sherri replied that she was down to her final edits of the last three chapters. In reality, the three chapters were still in her head, but she knew they'd go from brain to laptop fairly quick. It was only about seventy-five hundred to ten thousand words and if she put her mind to it, she'd be finished in two or three days of hard writing.

Sherri finished with her email and switched over to Facebook where she posted her sadness about ending her series and saying goodbye to her beloved characters. The saga had taken up four years of her life and her regular characters were like old friends in Sherri's mind. She hated to say goodbye to them. Perhaps she'd write some spin-off novellas. Her fans would love that, and she could use them as freebies at book signings.

She was rereading her outline for the final chapters when she heard a vehicle in the cinder drive. Sherri glanced at the time on her laptop and saw that it read twelve-fifty. She saved her work, powered down the machine, and closed it.

When she heard feet on the old porch, Sherri rested the laptop on the broad arm of the sofa and rose. Someone knocked and Sherri went to the door. She tugged the old, warped door open to find a tall, sturdily built man in his fifties standing on the porch. He was vaguely familiar, but Sherri couldn't place him.

I should know this guy. He looks to be about my age.

The patch sewn over his left breast pocket read DR with Realistic Renovations spelled out in red letters around the outside of the white patch.

He glanced down at his clipboard as Sherri opened the door. "Mrs. Lambert?" he asked with a hesitant smile beneath his full, reddish mustache. A few wrinkles at the corners of his bright, brown eyes were the only real marks of age on his handsome face.

"It's Ms., actually," Sherri corrected. "Please come in," she said and held the door open for him to enter.

Sherri guessed him to be about six-four and very well-built. He didn't have the paunch, protruding over his belt, many men in their mid-to late-fifties possessed. His brown hair was combed back from his forehead and clipped close around the ears and across the neck. As he walked past her to take in the room, Sherri saw he filled out his jeans nicely in the rear.

I've always liked a nice ass on a man.

"What exactly do you have in mind here?" he asked as he made his way into the dated kitchen. "Do you have any idea when the house was built and by whom?"

"I really have no idea," Sherri admitted and

shrugged her shoulders. "It was my grandparents' place, but I think they bought it already built back before the Depression. I'd planned to go to the library to do some research on it but haven't made it in yet."

"Try the county tax office first," he suggested. "They'd have the best information as to when the house was built from the tax records and such. Some of the places around here were built before the Indian Wars."

"Thanks," Sherri said, studying the man's face. "I'll do that as a starting point." He was so familiar, but she couldn't seem to place him. They were of a similar age. Maybe they'd gone to school together in Barrett. She glanced at the patch on his shirt again. DR, who did she know with those initials?

I should just ask. It'll drive me nuts until I figure it out.

"Realistic Renovations does mainly historic renovations of log cabins and big Victorians, but I'm sure we can update the place for you" he said as he studied the door frame between the kitchen and the small second bedroom cluttered with boxes she had yet to unpack from her California condo.

"I know," Sherri said. "It's why I contacted you. Follow me." She led him back through the living room and out onto the porch where she pulled up a piece of the old shingle siding to expose the chinked logs beneath.

"I found this after I moved back in here after my grandparents passed. The inside walls in the bedroom are like this too but covered with that godawful paneling. I imagine it's the same in the living room," she said with a scowl and wrinkled nose.

"My goodness," he said with a grin on his handsome, tanned face and then stepped back inside to study the wall where the gas space heater stood.

He tapped on the paneling a few times. His grin broadened and Sherri could see even, white teeth in his mouth. DR went back outside, walked off the end of the porch, and went to the outside of that same wall.

Sherri watched him grab at a piece of the siding and begin to lift it away. "Do you mind?" He asked but didn't wait for a reply before tugging away the old siding. "That's what I figured," he mumbled and tossed the piece of siding into the grass before tearing away another to reveal a wooden frame around an old fireplace built from the local reddish-gold sandstone. "You have yourself a nice fireplace behind that gas heater in there, ma'am," he said with a broad smile.

"Really?" Sherri gasped. "I lived here with my grandparents for years and never knew it was there. I don't even know that *they* knew it was there."

They had to know. They had that ugly paneling put up in the late sixties.

"Maybe not," DR said and shrugged his broad shoulders. This whole area was settled back in the early nineteenth century by families up from the Carolinas. They followed the rivers up here and settled because of the rich farmland and all the forests. The Indians were run out of the area after the Blackhawk Wars in 1838." He ran his hand through his hair and grinned.

I should have known that.

"We've done several of these old double cabins in the past few years."

Sherri followed him, admiring his behind, as he walked on around to the back of the house.

"See there," he said and pointed to the roofline. "This section was added on as a shed extension to make these two bedrooms off the back of the original cabin. The walls between the living areas and the bedrooms are more than likely log and were plastered over around the turn of the century."

He took a deep breath before continuing as they walked around and into the utility room off the kitchen. "I hope they only boarded over the fireplace inside and didn't plaster over the stones and fill in the firebox. That will take a lot of work to clean up if they did."

DR motioned toward the other end of the house with his big, tanned hand. "In that opening between the kitchen and the smaller bedroom would have been a fireplace with a hearth open to both sides. One side would have been used for cooking the meals there in the kitchen and the other for heating the sleeping areas in the back. That fireplace was probably taken out around the turn of the century when people started using iron cook stoves rather than open hearths."

He sure seems to know his history and is sure of himself. He's almost a little cocky about it, but I'm enjoying the history lesson.

"I know the bathroom off the kitchen was built by closing in that end of the porch," Sherri said and pointed to the door on the other side of the big kitchen. "I remember how my grandfather had a heck of a time getting up under the floor to fix a plumbing problem once," she said with a sad chuckle.

They walked out the back door and around to the front of the house, where DL studied the stone foundation beneath the bathroom. "So, what would you like to do with this place, Ms. Lambert? It has a lot of potential for a historic renovation."

"I think I'd like to take it back as close to its original state as possible with the modern conveniences to make it livable, of course." She chuckled. "I can't see myself living without electricity or indoor plumbing," Sherri said with a smile and a slight shrug of her shoulders as he laughed along with her.

He has such a nice smile and his laugh sounds so familiar. I'm sure I know this guy.

"What's your experience been with these things?" she asked.

"Do you want my personal opinion, or the company upsell?" he asked with a grin and a raised bushy eyebrow.

"Yours, please," Sherri said as she bent and pulled a dandelion from the bed of wilting poppies against the foundation. "You seem to be very knowledgeable. I appreciate all the history. I can tell you enjoy the work."

"Thanks," he said with an embarrassed grin. He turned back to the house and pointed. "Well, the first thing you're gonna want to do is strip it down to the bare bones; get rid of the carpet, the paneling, and all the modern fixtures, windows, and doors. They make very energy-efficient windows and doors now that look like the period ones."

He put his hand on the old siding and smiled. "We'll need to rip all that framing away from around the fireplace and clean it up too. You'll want to have the flue cleaned and get it all working properly again if you plan to use it," he said, "and you should. They probably just boarded up the firebox, so that won't be a hard fix, but we'll have to patch it in where they bored the hole for the gas heater's exhaust."

Sherri nodded in agreement. "That sounds good to me. I have some magazines and catalogues in the kitchen with some ideas I've marked. Would you like some coffee and have a look?"

Who the hell is this guy? He looks so familiar.

"Sure," he said and followed Sherri into the kitchen where he took a seat and began leafing through the magazines, stopping at the pages she had marked. Sherri watched him nodding his head as he studied the pages after putting on a pair of horn-rimmed reading glasses.

They give him a very distinguished look.

Sherri started another pot of coffee, got out a package of Pecan Sandies, and put them onto a plate.

"You have some good ideas here," he told her and glanced up at the ceiling. "What do you want to do with the ceiling?"

Sherri shrugged her shoulders. "I know this is probably full of blown-in insulation. Do you think we should take it all down and open it up?"

"We can do that," he said with a grin and Sherri knew she was about to get the company up-sell. "We can use insulated panels against the outside roof and then overlay those with tongue and groove planking stained to match the logs."

"You'd recommend leaving the log walls, then, and not insulating them?"

"Not much sense having a log house if you can't see the logs," he said and winked. "You should have them sanded, of course, patch any missing chinking, and then stained if you don't like the color. You can use drywall on the inside walls if you want to break it up, but I'd leave the outside walls natural with the logs showing."

He took a deep breath as Sherri filled his coffee cup. "I'm not gonna lie to you, ma'am. These renovations are pricey. There's a lot of labor involved."

Not the up-sale I'd have figured.

"I expected that," Sherri admitted. "I have some funds set aside for the project. I sold my condo in

Palm Springs and have some cash coming from that."

"I can't imagine why you'd want to leave a place like Palm Springs to move here," he said with a disgusted sneer. "Won't you miss actual civilization?"

"You've obviously never been to Palm Springs in August," Sherri said, rolled her eyes, and grinned. "It's like Dante's lowest level of hell."

He laughed. "I flew in there once," he said, "but I was going up to the Yucca Valley area on a project."

"Yucca is nice in the summer, but it sits up at about four-thousand feet above sea level. Palm Springs is down almost at sea-level and in a bowl. Too damned hot and dry. If you don't mind shades of brown," Sherri said, shaking her head, "it's all right, but I missed the green and the changing seasons. Out there you get warm, hot, and hotter for seasons."

"I suppose," he sighed, "but I think I'd do just about anything to get away from here again and if I did, I certainly wouldn't want to be coming back."

Who are you?

"Are you from here or are you a transplant?" she asked and studied his familiar face again.

"Born and raised," he sighed. "I left for a while to go to college in Tennessee and met my wife there," he said sadly, "but it didn't work out and I came back to look after my mom when she got sick. How about you?"

Married, but divorced. I wonder if he's remarried?

"I've been gone from the area for almost thirty years," she told him, "but decided to come back after my grandparents died and left me this place."

"You never married?"

Sherri smiled and gave an amused snort. "Three

times, but it never took. I don't think Happily-Ever-After was meant for me. I started using my maiden name again after my first divorce and never changed it again. Not an optimist, I suppose."

He laughed uneasily, pulled his clipboard up in front of him, and began making some notes. "I see you have Victorian-style bathroom fixtures marked in your books here. Is that what you have in mind?"

"Have you looked at that Pepto-Bismol mess in there?" Sherri asked and jerked her head toward the bathroom door. "It's a freaking disaster."

He chuckled and raised an eyebrow. "If you'll let us recover the tiles and fixtures for clean-up, we'll offer you a good trade toward what you want to replace them with."

"Are you serious?" Sherri asked incredulously. "You'd really want that ugly crap?"

DR rolled his eyes. "Mid-century Modern is all the rage right now, and you've got everything in there if we can get it out without messing it up. You've even got the matching floor and it looks to be in like-new condition with no chipped or broken tiles."

"Yah," Sherri sighed sadly, "Granny loved her ugly pink bathroom and took good care of it. I think they had it all put in while my mom was pregnant with me back in late '57 or early '58. You know, the I Love Lucy era." She saw DR smile and give her an odd look before going back to his paperwork.

He pulled a couple of papers off the clipboard and handed them to her before he stood. "Here are some rough figures for the labor costs for doing the basic strip down. We can do more solid figures once we know what we have under the siding, paneling, and carpet." He extended his hand and Sherri took it.

"Look that over and give us a call to let us know

when you'd like to get started." He drained his coffee cup and turned toward the door.

He looks good walking away in a pair of jeans, that's for sure.

Sherri followed him and watched the man get into his truck. When he'd turned out of the drive, she looked down at the papers for the first time. At the bottom of the page she saw a signature. Dylan Roberts.

Oh, my god, Dilly freaking Roberts? The hottest hunk from our high school class and the biggest stuck up asshole of the Snot Squad? His daddy was a big-time Barrett attorney and he was one of that privileged class in school who wouldn't have given a low-rent country girl like me a second thought. He probably didn't even recognize my name, much less my face today.

In exasperation, Sherri tossed the papers onto the table and began cleaning up their coffee cups.

I knew I should have recognized him. He sat right next to me in sophomore English and copied my work all year. I even wrote a dozen papers for him. What an ass.

❧ 3 ❧

D ylan adjusted his behind in his seat as he traveled down the bumpy, gravel road to the blacktop to take him the few miles back into Barrett.

Wow, Sherri Lambert. I wondered what had become of her after high school. I knew she lived out in the sticks some- where, but who'd have thought it would be in that house. Why did it have to be that damned house?

His phone chimed and he glanced down to see it was the office number. "DR," he answered.

"Hey, Dilly," his brother Bob said. Bob and his mother were the only people allowed to call him Dilly anymore. He'd outgrown the childish bas- tardization of Dylan with high school and after he'd come back to Barrett, he'd insisted people call him DR if not Dylan.

"What's up, Bobby?" Dylan used the childish ver- sion of his brother's name to remind him Dylan didn't like him using Dilly in the office in front of the other employees.

"Did you make that Lambert appointment? When I talked to her about the appointment, she sounded excited about a complete renovation on her place. Is it gonna be a money-maker for us?"

Of course, I made the appointment, asshole. I never miss appointments..

Bob Roberts ran the office part of Realistic Renovations, while Dylan did the grunt work and managed the crews. Bob had an MBA and Dylan a degree in Structural Engineering with a minor in History. It had been a perfect fit for the two brothers to form their business.

"Yah," Dylan told his brother, "I made it out there and I think we'll get the project. I gave her some figures to chew on, and I'll call her back in a day or two to see what she wants to do with it."

"Cool," Bob said, "We can use another good project and this one is close to home, so we won't have travel expenses. Let me look at your figures when you get back to the office, and I'll have the contracts typed up, so you'll have them with you the next time you meet with her."

There was a long pause and Dylan heard his brother shuffling papers. "Was it the Sherri Lambert we went to school with?"

Dylan rolled his eyes, knowing where his brother's mind was going. It's where it always went. "Yah, it was her."

His brother chuckled. "You get a little while you were out there, bro? Sherri used to really put out, as I recall."

"Don't be silly, Bob. We're not in high school anymore."

"A leopard doesn't change its spots, bro or is she a cougar now," Bob said with a lascivious giggle. "If you play your cards right you might be able to get a taste of that during your lunch breaks but watch the other guys. We don't wanna be paying them while they're pullin' a train. Is she still hot?"

His brother's lewd remarks disgusted Dylan and

he very nearly disconnected. "Not everybody is like you and has sex on the brain, Bobby," Dylan snapped. "If you want this project, you'd better show her some respect. She wants a full reno and it could be a big payday for the company." Dylan didn't wait for a reply from his brother and disconnected.

What an ass. I can't believe we came from the same womb sometimes.

Dylan drove on into town with high school and his life forty years ago on his mind. The song *Glory Days* came on the radio and Dylan turned it off with an agitated punch of the button on the dash. High School had definitely been Dylan Roberts' glory days. He'd been first-string on the basketball team, helping to take the Barrett High team to State in both his Junior and Senior years.

His academics had been good, though teachers knew he had to have good grades to stay on the team and Dylan knew some had given him grades he probably hadn't deserved. He'd dated the prettiest cheerleaders and been homecoming king twice.

With his coach's help, Dylan had won a basketball scholarship to Tennessee State, but an accident on the court during a pre-season practice had blown out his knee before Dylan had a chance to play his first college game, ending his college basketball career.

The school had honored the scholarship for the first year, however, and his father, along with student loans, had paid his tuition for the next three years and Dylan had managed an education at a good school.

There had been plenty of fraternity parties, but Dylan hadn't enjoyed the same acclaim in college he had in high school. The college cheerleaders wouldn't give him the time of day and unlike high school, the instructors at Tennessee State actually expected him to earn his grades. It had been eye-opening and difficult, but with hard work and study, Dylan had earned a degree and even went on into a graduate program in engineering.

He started dating a girl from an affluent Mississippi plantation family he met at a fraternity party, and they married very soon after graduating because Tammy was pregnant. Her father thought Dylan, the son of a small-town attorney, was beneath Tammy and hadn't made their seven-year marriage easy.

Tammy gave birth to a daughter they named Carla Jean and after a difficult pregnancy had refused to go through it again. She pushed Dylan into a vasectomy he hadn't wanted. He then had to endure years of ridicule from his father about not producing a son to carry on the Roberts family name.

After seven rocky years, he and Tammy divorced. Carla Jean, the light of his life, stayed with her mother and grandparents on the plantation, and Dylan moved to a couple of different cities before returning to Barrett to help with his ailing mother.

Life in Barrett wasn't what Dylan remembered, though. His high school buddies had gone off to college or moved on with wives and children. The cheerleaders were married now or had moved away. He screwed around some but found nothing meaningful.

Returning to Barrett had been depressing until his brother Bobby came back to town after his own divorce and their mother had fallen ill with breast cancer. Their father had begun suffering from dementia and had to be institutionalized. The brothers knew they'd have to take on the responsibility of their ailing mother and moved back into their childhood home.

Living at home with mom doesn't exactly make for an easy love-life.

One afternoon, while sitting with their mother, watching a home improvement program, the idea for Realistic Renovations had been born. Their first project had been their mother's home, a big Craftsman, built in the 1930s. It had turned out well and Bobby had arranged a photo shoot with local newspapers.

He used the publication of those articles to coincide with the announcement of the opening of Realistic Renovations. It had been a genius marketing move and the company had hit the ground running.

In their first year, they made more money than either brother could have imagined and continued to make yearly monetary gains.

If I could rein Bobby in a little, things might be okay, but if I can't, I don't know what I'm going to do.

Bobby used the media to their advantage with big spreads in the papers with their latest projects decorated for the holidays as they would have been in the period the house was built. Their mother's health improved, and their business flourished. Life was good, though Dylan couldn't help but feel something was missing.

Dylan had loved the history and been eager to branch away from Craftsman homes and Victorians into renovating log cabins like Sherri's. He'd traveled to Texas and other western states to study renovated log homes. The business had taken Dylan's mind off his dismal personal life, but then he runs into Sherri Lambert on a job and it had all come flooding back.

She is still hot, and she still makes me laugh. I forgot how she always made me laugh. She's older, sure, but aren't we all.

Maybe I should ask her out. Hell, I'm almost sixty years old and haven't dated in decades. What would we do on a damned date? Barrett isn't exactly a hot date destination. There's not even a damned movie theatre in town anymore. Dinner and a few drinks at Applebee's? Get a few drinks in her and take her home for a little fun in her bedroom?

Hell, I don't even know if my damned thing would work with a real woman anymore. It only gets used when I self-serve in the shower these days.

Dylan's mind wandered back to high school again. Sherri Lambert had been in a few classes with him. He remembered that she was smart. She'd let him copy her homework a few times and had even written an English paper or two for him.

He'd always thought Sherri was nice with a great sense of humor, but he'd never have considered dating her back then. She was a country girl, not a townie or in the right crowd to make him look good.

Dylan remembered one of his cheerleader girl-friends making fun of Sherri's dress one day because it had obviously been homemade. He'd laughed too and as he remembered the hurt look he'd caught on the younger Sherri's face, Dylan was suddenly ashamed of his younger self.

I was such an ass. Why wouldn't I have asked her out back then? Because she was from the country and screwed around a little? As I recall, we were all screwing around as much as we could back then. Hell, I remember Mom calling Bobby a fucking man-slut after he came down with his second case of the clap his Junior year.

Dylan parked in front of their small, rented office, pulled the cost sheet he'd scribbled for Sherri's project from his clipboard, and got out of his truck.

Bobby was on the phone when he stepped into his office but cut the call short when he saw Dylan.

"Are those the figures for the Lambert job?"

Dylan tossed the papers on Bobby's cluttered desk. "Yep. She's talking about a full top to bottom cabin renovation. It's just a small two-bedroom with one bath, but it has a nice fireplace and what I saw of the logs beneath the sidings look good."

"The floors?"

"Lino in the kitchen and carpet," Dylan said, "but they felt firm."

"And the bathroom?"

Dylan smiled. "You're gonna love this," he said. "She's got a complete retro in pink and black. The floor is even tiled with those little hexagons. It's beautiful."

"That doesn't fit very well in a pioneer cabin renovation."

"She hates it and wants it gone." Dylan smiled. "I told her we'd give her a good trade out on it."

Bobby raised a brow. "Not too good, I hope. We can't afford to give away the farm here, bro." Bobby frowned at his older brother. "We can't be taking the job in trade. We need cash money to get through the winter season."

Yah and I know exactly where that cash money will be going, bro.

"Like I said before, Bob," Dylan said. "This could be the project to see this company through the winter, so be respectful of the lady. She has cash. We won't have to deal with fucking bank inspectors on this one."

"Well, that's something at least." Bobby smiled. "She's got money, huh?"

Well, that got your damned attention.

"Said she sold a condo in Palm Springs. She sounded like she's flush."

"Must have hooked a rich old geezer out there," Bobby said with a grin.

Dylan shrugged. "You know as much as I do, but she wants everything back to the way it was, so figure doors, windows, metal roof, and insulated plank in the attic."

"You got it," he said and winked again. "I'll pad it well for incidentals."

❃ 4 ❃

"Come on, Molly Doll," he said, and his breath smelled of stale liquor, "give daddy what he needs tonight." She felt his fingers groping painfully into her crotch.

"I'm trying to sleep, sweetie," she complained. "It's late and I'm tired." She tried to roll over onto her side again, but he yanked her flat and pressed her shoulders into the lumpy mattress.

"I said I want a little of this pussy," he growled angrily and stared down at her. "Get your hand down there and play with him a little to get him nice and hard so I can fuck you."

He yanked her right hand to his naked crotch, and she began to caress his flaccid penis. She knew it would be of no use and gave a mental groan. He'd come home drunk again. If she managed to get him hard at all, it wouldn't last, and he'd be angry with her again.

"Sure, baby," she whispered as she ran her fingers over his stiffening cock and then through the coarse hair and down over his hanging balls. He liked having his ball sack tickled lightly with her fingernails.

"Yah, Molly Doll," he sighed and blew his rancid breath into her face, "do it the way your daddy likes it." He nuzzled into her neck and bit at the soft skin there. "You smell good, Doll—like honeysuckles. I like that.

She looked up to see his heavy-lidded brown eyes half-closed as he concentrated on achieving a full erection.

Why can't it be like it used to be before he started sampling his own product so much? It used to be so good with us. When he's sober, he's such a sweet and loving man.

"You've got it now, Molly Doll," he sighed, and she cringed away from the smell of stale cigarette smoke and alcohol on his breath. "Stroke daddy's dick the way he likes it and then he's gonna use your sweet, wet pussy to stroke it with."

Why does he insist on calling himself my daddy? He knows I hate that. He's not my father and I certainly wouldn't bed with him if he was. It's disgusting and vile.

She spread her legs a little wider to invite him in and brought her long, shapely legs up to wrap around his waist. He accepted her invitation and rammed his erection into her pussy. He thrust vigorously at first but lost his erection after only a few minutes. She glanced up to see fury in his dark eyes as he glowered down at her.

"I don't know why you make me do this, Molly Doll," he snarled and then drew his arm back and slapped her hard.

The sting of it brought tears to her eyes, but she was thankful he's used the flat of his hand this time and not his fist. He smacked her twice more, and the sound of his hand on her flesh brought his erection back to life.

She brought her hands up and began to gently run her fingernails in circles over his back as she flexed the muscles in her pussy to massage his reawakening dick.

"Is that better, daddy?" she cooed softly and sucked one of his nipples into her mouth to tease with her tongue.

The rest of it was rough. He liked it rough when he'd been drinking. He popped out of her pussy a time or two and shoved the head into her asshole, stretching it past her capacity to endure and she flinched away and yelped in pain. That made him harder and he finally returned to her pussy to finish.

"Here it comes, Molly Doll," he bellowed atop her. "Daddy's gonna fill up that tight little pussy tonight. Oh, yaaahh," he groaned with his release. "Oh, hell yah," he groaned as he shoved his dick deep into her.

He never cares if I get mine anymore. It's always all about him. I wonder if all men are like that.

He dropped down atop her, panting in her ear. She waited until his heart slowed and his pants became soft snores before she rolled him off her and pulled the sheet up over his naked body. She sat up to stare at her reflection in the faint light of the rising sun coming through the bedside window.

She touched her cheeks gingerly and hoped they wouldn't be bruised again. She was almost out of pancake and didn't have much money squirreled away to buy more yet. She ran a hand through her short curly bob. She missed her longer hair, but this short style was all the rage now. All the queens of the silver screen were wearing theirs this way. Hair grows back and she had to admit that this was much easier to take care of.

Sherri woke sitting on the edge of the bed and grabbed at the mattress to keep from tumbling to the floor.

I don't remember sitting up.

She glanced into the mirror and her head began to swim. It wasn't her face staring back at her. It was the face of the blonde.

Am I still dreaming?

The room was different, as well. The furniture wasn't hers. It was of an older style. Sherri blinked to clear her head, but when she opened her eyes the odd furniture hadn't changed.

How can I still be dreaming? I'm sitting up.

It was the furniture from her dream—the blonde girl's furniture. She turned her head to glance down at the spot on the mattress beside her and let out a relieved sigh. Sherri half expected to see a sleeping man there, but it was empty.

Sherri squeezed her eyes tight again and massaged her throbbing temples.

What the hell is going on? Who wakes up with a damned headache?

When Sherri opened her eyes again, her furniture had returned, and the morning breeze blew the curtains out into the room with a hint of honeysuckle wafting in on the breeze from the nearby hedge.

It was just the damned dream. I wasn't awake yet. This is so damned strange. I can't remember sitting up, but I remember the girl in my dream sitting up, though.

Sherri reached for her robe and tugged it on over her chilled shoulders. She snugged it at the waist and trudged out of the bedroom, through the living room, and into the dark kitchen where she filled the coffee pot and popped a bagel into the toaster.

I should probably have bacon and eggs. My diet is probably the reason for the crazy damned dreams and this headache.

Then she made her way into the bathroom and flipped on the light. In the mirror, Sherri noticed her cheeks were pink and she shuddered, remembering the stinging slaps from the man in her dream. She let her robe drop to the floor before sitting on the toilet to relieve herself. When Sherri wiped, the paper came away slimy with an oddly familiar aroma. She brought it closer to her nose and inhaled.

It's semen. How can that possibly be? I haven't had sex in over a year. This is fucking impossible. It wasn't even a good wet dream. I didn't cum.

Suddenly feeling cheated, Sherri dropped the slimy paper into the toilet after staring at it closely and flushed. It must have been some odd vaginal discharge.

She'd get online after her coffee and find a local gynecologist and make an appointment. She was due for a check-up, anyhow, and needed a local doctor. Maybe her body was trying to tell her something.

Sherri made her way back into the kitchen, poured some coffee, and buttered her bagel. Sherri sat at the table and shivered as she thought back on the oddly realistic dream.

Maybe my body is trying to tell me that it's been too damned long without a man between my legs. I write erotic scenes almost every day and get my body all worked up, but I don't have any actual physical release. That can't be healthy.

She took a long swallow of the hot, rich coffee and then went into the living room for her laptop. Back at the table with her coffee and buttered bagel, Sherri opened the Toshiba, checked her email, and did a quick scan of her Facebook page for messages and interesting posts from friends and family. She frowned when she saw a prodding message from her editor there, as well.

I had better get on this before they start asking for their advance back.

Motivated, Sherri checked her battery life, carried the laptop and coffee with her out to the thinly padded porch swing, and made herself comfortable for a few hours of serious writing. It was early Fall and after the sun burned off the morning chill, the day was comfortable. She turned off her phone so nobody would interrupt her concentration and she began to write.

When her screen flashed that she was down to ten percent battery, five hours had passed. Sherri had knocked out nearly two chapters and close to five thousand words. It was close to noon, so she carried the laptop inside, plugged it in, and went into the kitchen for a glass of ice water and a banana.

I should probably have some protein, but I don't have anything but fruit in the house. I'm even out of yogurt.

Two hours and three thousand words later, Sherri pressed the button on her laptop to send her finished manuscript off to her waiting editor.

She clicked her phone back on, and it immediately began chiming with messages. She checked her log and saw that she had missed two calls from her agent, one from her girlfriend in Palm Springs, and a text from Realistic Renovations.

Sherri checked the text first.

RR: I know I said I'd give you a couple of days, but I have some other figures I'd like to talk to you about. Would you let me buy you breakfast tomorrow? You can call me at this number or just text.

SL: Sure, breakfast sounds great. Where and when?
Her phone chimed in reply only a few minutes later.

RR: Is nine too early for you? Do you have a preference of a restaurant here in town?

SL: Is Pike's still open and do they still serve those glorious cream-cheese-filled pancakes?

RR: They are, and they do. I'll see you at Pike's at nine in the morning. Thx!

Wait, did Dylan Roberts just ask me out to breakfast? Would that be considered a date or a business meeting?

Sherri returned the call from her friend in Palm Springs but got her voicemail and tagged her with a 'you're it'. Between both their schedules, that could go on for days before they actually spoke. If it had been important, Kelly would have left a more detailed message or a 911 text.

Close to five in New York, Sherri called her agent's private number.

"Hi, this is Inga. How may I help you?"

"Hi, Inga. This is Sherri Lambert," Sherri replied and after a nervous pause, she added, "Whiskey Treat."

I hate that she never remembers my real name. I'm Sherri not Whiskey, though I suppose it's Whiskey who makes her money.

"Yes, of course, I'm so sorry, Ms. Lambert. I was just calling to inquire after the third book in your series. Have you delivered it to the publisher yet? If you have, I'll get after them for our next advance check," she said with a chuckle.

"I sent it off this afternoon and cc'd you. It should be in your inbox as we speak. It's the final book in the series, so I wouldn't be looking for any more advance checks just yet."

"I'm aware of that," Inga said in her clipped east

coast accent. "Have you given any consideration to your next project? Weren't you talking about a paranormal thing a few months ago?"

"Yah," Sherri sighed. "I've worked up some outlines and character sketches already, but I've never written in that genre before and I don't know how it would go over with my regular readers."

"Excellent. Send me over a synopsis of what you have in mind and I'll give it a read and run it by the publisher." Sherri heard the agent take a deep breath before continuing. "I'm sure they'll love it. You've developed a broad fan base over the past few years. Well, you've seen the fan mail."

"You don't think they'll want more of the same?" Sherri asked nervously. "The last three were Westerns. Won't the publisher want more Westerns?"

"They might, but your work has been very well received, Whiskey," Inga said confidently. "I'm sure they'll love whatever you have in mind and just shift it over to one of their other imprints. Paranormal has a huge audience." She took a breath and added, "As long as there's a romantic storyline with a happy ending they can keep it with their Hearts and Flowers imprint and your readers are more likely to find it."

"Actually," Sherri said, "I was thinking about beginning the story in the nineteenth century and then moving the series along into the present day with a romantic storyline in each one."

"That sounds interesting, but you're not thinking about doing one of those Outlander-type time travel things, I hope," Inga groaned.

"No," Sherri said with a chuckle. "It's been done to death now. I was thinking about starting the story with characters before the Civil War and then moving the story along with other characters in closer time periods until the story winds up in the present."

"And what would be paranormal about that?"

"How about evil witches, horrible curses, and nasty ghosts?"

"Sounds doable," Inga said with a chuckle. "Send me a detailed synopsis with what you have and your character sketches. I'll run it all past Karen and see if I can get you a handsome advance."

You mean get us a handsome advance. You skim your fifteen percent right off the top.

"That sounds good," Sherri said. "I'll try to make it pretty and shoot it off to you tonight."

"Excellent. I'll be looking forward to seeing what you have, and I know Karen will be too."

Excellent, indeed. If I'm gonna be rebuilding this place, my bank account is gonna need a serious cash injection.

❋ 5 ❋

Dylan sat in his truck parked in the little gravel parking lot outside Pike's Diner, waiting for Sherri to arrive. He glanced at his phone to check the time again. He was early, but he wanted to be here in the parking lot when Sherri arrived.

Why am I so damned nervous? This isn't a date; it's a business meeting.

He saw her electric-blue PT Cruiser turn into the lot and he smiled.

It's a damned cute car but stands out like a sore thumb in sleepy little Barrett.

Dylan watched her get out of the car and smiled. She still had a nice ass and her boobs looked great in the tight sweater. He waited until she shut the door to get out of his truck.

"Hi, Ms. Lambert," he called and waved.

Should I call her Sherri? We were in school together.

Sherri turned and a smile spread across her pretty face. She stopped and waited for him to join her so they could walk into the old diner together. He watched her tuck a red curl behind her ear.

She always did that when she was nervous. Is she nervous about meeting me?

Inside, the aroma of fried bacon and stale cigarette smoke hit their noses. It was common in every greasy spoon across the country and Dylan smiled. Pike's had been one of his favorite places to eat since childhood and he was glad Sherri had suggested it. Choosing it over the more expensive restaurant at the Best Western by the highway said loads about the woman in Dylan's way of thinking. She wasn't pretentious and wouldn't take advantage of a man by choosing an expensive restaurant for a free meal.

They took seats at an empty table near the back of the narrow room. The waitress, who looked to be about their age, brought them menus encased in red plastic, dingy and sticky with years of greasy fingers handling them.

"Hey, Dil," the waitress said as she filled their cups with coffee. She gave Sherri a quick glance before returning to Dylan with a smile on her plump face. "What can I get you guys today?"

"I think we both want the stuffed pancakes and sausage, Candi, and two coffees."

The waitress glanced at Sherri and she nodded her approval. "You comin' over to the Westie on Saturday, Dil?" she asked Dylan as she scribbled on her order pad.

"I don't know yet," Dylan replied and shrugged his broad shoulders. "Who else is coming?"

"Probably everybody," she said with a girlish giggle. "It's Kitty's birthday this month, so the whole gang should be there."

I hate those stupid things. They're so boring. I've heard the same stupid stories dozens of times.

"I'll think about it," he said and picked up his coffee.

"Ok, I'll have this out in a bit," the waitress said and shuffled off toward the kitchen.

"A bunch of us get together once a month at the Best Western for dinner and drinks," Dylan explained. "We celebrate whoever's birthday happens to fall that month. I guess this month's is Kitty Jackson's ... it used to be Kathy Hill. She started using Kitty in college before she married Jimmy Jackson."

Sherri remembered Kathy Hill and Jimmy Jackson. They were both part of his old clique and the stuck-up crowd everyone else called the Snot Squad at Barrett High. Sherri stared after the departing waitress with a questioning look in her eyes.

He'd called her Candi. Would she recognize that chubby waitress as Candi Wyatt? In school, Candi had been a petite little thing and always dressed in the latest fashions. She'd been a cheerleader at Barrett High and Dylan Robert's steady girlfriend for several years. Her father had owned a farm machinery dealership and her mother a beauty salon with tanning beds in the back.

"Was that Candi Wyatt?" Sherri asked Dylan uneasily.

"Yah," Dylan said with the shadow of a grin on his face. "The years haven't been very good to Candi and her family. Her old man committed suicide and her mom's the town drunk now."

"Oh my," Sherri sighed. "What happened?"

"When the economy tanked a few years ago, Candi's dad went bankrupt and lost his big tractor dealership. He snapped and ..." Dylan put a finger to his head in imitation of a gun.

"Then her mom lost her shop downtown and she just went sorta nuts, too. She was a bit of a social climber, you know, and when people in town started shunning her, she turned to the bottle." Dylan rolled his eyes. "She's a sloppy drunk, too, and shows up places smashed. Candi's had a hard time of it and her husband isn't much help."

"Who did she marry?" Sherri asked.

"Terry Clem," Dylan said and took a sip of coffee.

"The pot dealer?" Sherri asked in wide-eyed surprise.

Terry Clem had been the go-to guy in Barrett if you wanted pot back in their high school days and the last guy anyone would have expected Candi Wyatt to have ended up with.

"The same," Dylan said in a hushed tone, "but he's graduated from pot to meth now. He owns that old trailer park north of town and they're all cook houses now except for the big doublewide he and Candi live in."

"Wow," Sherri said. "I certainly wouldn't have thought of Terry Clem. He was such a … a …"

"Scumbag?" Dylan added, but quieted when he saw Candi coming with their plates of food in her hands.

Candi set the plates in front of them but stood staring at Sherri intently. "I know who you are, now," Candi gasped, staring at Sherri with her eyes wide.

Oh, shit, here it comes. Candi never liked Sherri because she was smart and got the good grades Candi didn't.

"How 'bout a little more coffee," Dylan said to redirect Candi from wherever she was headed with Sherri. He was in no mood for one of Candi's silly rants.

"You're Whiskey Treat, the writer," Candi said exuberantly. "I've read all your books. Wait," she said and rushed away from their table toward the kitchen.

"Whiskey Treat?" Dylan queried with a deep furrow in his brow.

"I'm a writer now," Sherri said. "My agent

thought Whiskey Treat would be a better pen name than Sherri Lambert." She grinned and shrugged her shoulders. "It's all about selling more books, after all."

"Do you?" he asked with a raised a thick brow. "Sell books?"

Candi came rushing back to the table with a paperback book clutched in her hands. "Will you sign this to Candi, please, Miss Treat?" She held the ragged book out to Sherri who recognized it as one of her first, *Lost Hope*, about a woman who grew up in a small town and struggled in high school.

"I can't believe a real famous author is sittin' right here in our little diner here in Barrett. How do you know her Dylan?"

Sherri opened the book, took the pen offered by Candi and signed it, but beneath Whiskey Treat she signed her real name, Sherri Lambert. Candi grabbed the book back when Sherri handed it to her, and Dylan watched the waitress' face fall as she read the inscription and the signatures.

"You're … Sherri Lambert?" Candi gasped as she stared into Sherri's face and then turned the book over to stare at the author's photo on the ragged back cover. "Wow, I guess you *are* her."

"I'm glad you like the books," Sherri said as she forked up some of the cream-cheese-filled pancakes.

Candi stuffed the book into the pocket of her grease-stained smock, turned, and marched away without uttering another word.

"I hope you don't have that effect on all your fans," Dylan said with an impish grin.

"Yah, me too," Sherri said and returned his grin.

"So, you write books, Sherri?" he asked, using her first name for the first time.

"Erotic Romance novels," she said with an

impish grin. "Most are set in the Old West, but I did a few contemporaries when I first started out."

He raised an eyebrow. "Erotic, huh?"

I'm gonna have to check some of those out.

They finished their meal chatting about classmates; where they were now and those who were no longer around at all. It had been forty years since their graduation and several of the people who'd graduated with them had passed away. Many had passed from natural causes while others had suffered accidents, committed suicide, and one had even been murdered. Several had moved away from Barrett and some had gone to prison.

They didn't get their coffee cups refilled either. Dylan had to wait at the register for the other waitress to get their check from Candi who was nowhere to be seen until they were about to step outside.

She came storming from the kitchen with Sherri's book clutched in her hand "You, hateful bitch," she snarled as she waved the book at them. "Hope, Colorado, is actually Barrett. Isn't it? And I suppose Cindy *Wyant* is supposed to be me? Not very original there, Sherri," she sneered. "She's a blonde like me, her dad owns a *car* dealership, and her mom runs a dress shop downtown? Could you be any more transparent?"

When she saw Dylan holding back a grin, she hurled the book at him. "Don't laugh, Dilly, because Cindy's boyfriend, *Billy,*" she said, glaring at Sherri, "is a real dumbass in that damned book of hers."

He caught the book as Candi stormed off back toward the kitchen. The woman at the register stretched her hand out to Dylan for the book with a smile tugging at the corners of her bright-red mouth.

"I've read that book, honey," she said to Sherri, grinning. "If that bitch Cindy is supposed to be our

Candi, then you hit the nail square on the head with her." She turned her attention to Dylan, narrowed her eyes, and pointed a talon-like finger. "If you were her model for that Billy, then you should be ashamed of yourself, young man."

Dylan held the door open for Sherri as they stepped out into the bright morning sun. "I guess I'm gonna have to buy that damned book."

After leaving Pike's, Sherri drove to the county tax office and found that her house had been recorded as having been built prior to 1838 when Jasper had first been designated as an official county by the state. That was as far back as their records went and the clerk suggested she visit the archivist at the public library for further information, if she needed it.

Sherri drove to the redbrick building that housed the public library in Barrett and went inside. A pretty, young woman sat at the counter, and when Sherri asked to see the archivist about some information on her property, the woman picked up the phone and asked someone to come up front.

As she waited, she inhaled the aroma of books. Sherri remembered spending hours in this building as a youngster, searching for interesting books to read. Books had been her escape from reality for as long as Sherri could remember—first as a reader and now as a writer.

"May I help you?" a man's voice said, and Sherri turned to see a vaguely familiar face.

She extended her hand. "I'm Sherri Lambert and I need to do some research on my grandparents' property just outside the city limits. I have all the property numbers and stuff from the tax office."

He took her hand in his and smiled. "I haven't seen you since school, Sherri. How've you been?" He must have recognized the uncertainty on her face. "Louis Cummings," he said as he shook her hand.

"Of course, I'm sorry, Louis. It's been a while, and I've been away from Barrett for a very long time. I see faces that seem familiar but can't place names. It's a little embarrassing."

"I wish I could say the same about being away," he said with a sad smile. "I was born in Barrett and will die here, no doubt."

Sherri nodded. "You're an archivist?"

"That I am. I always enjoyed history and my granddad got me into the exciting local history with stories about when he was a kid growing up around Barrett. When I went to college, I studied the history of our fine state and focused on this part of it."

Sherri followed him to a small office down the hall past the restrooms. She recalled that it had once housed copy machines and the library's projection equipment for presentations.

He moved a stack of books off a chair and set them on the floor beside others. "Won't you have a seat?"

"Thanks," she said and sat down in the sixties-era office chair upholstered in faded orange burlap-type fabric.

"Now what do you have for me and what do you want to know?"

Sherri took a file folder from her purse and passed it across the desk to Louis. She told him about the logs she'd found beneath the shingle siding and that she was having it renovated by Dylan's company.

"They do excellent work," he told her as he studied the numbers on her papers. "They renovated that big, run-down Victorian across from the high school and now it's a Bed and Breakfast of some acclaim in the state."

Sherri watched him stand and run his fingers over a plat map of the county. "Here you are," he said and pointed to a spot on the map. He then pulled a big book from a shelf behind his desk and leafed through the pages until he finally stopped and ran his finger down a page.

"It says here the land your house is built on was settled by Hiram and Millie Aiken in or about 1820."

He looked up from the book with a broad smile on his face. "If you have their actual cabin there, Sherri, you have a significant piece of county and state history. The Aikens traveled here from Carolina and were some of the earliest pioneer families in this part of our state."

"Wow," Sherri said, echoing his excitement.

❧ 6 ❧

Sherri stopped by their office and signed the contracts with Realistic Renovations for a full restoration of her cabin and they began the work of stripping the place down almost immediately.

"We've got crews sitting idle right now," Dylan told her as he helped his men drag ladders off the truck. "They'd rather be working and so would I."

"And Bobby would like to see my money become his money," Sherri said with a grin. She'd written him a large check to get things moving a few days before.

"That he would," Dylan said with a deep chuckle. "That he would." Sherri walked with him as he hefted the big ladder onto his shoulder and carried it to the house where part of the crew would begin removing the shingle siding from the structure while the others worked inside, stripping the floors and walls.

This is gonna be a hell of a mess.

It surprised her to hear men with hammers inside, already prying off the window casings and floor moldings so they could begin pulling up the carpet and ripping the old paneling from the walls.

Sherri had to admit she was eager to see the old house stripped down to its bare bones.

I can't wait to see what it looked like when Granny and Paw-Paw first moved in here.

"Your guys get right to it," Sherri said and put a hand over her nose and mouth as they walked back inside where dust had already begun to fill the air in the little house.

"We takin' this old carpet to the dump in town, boss?" One of the younger members of the crew asked Dylan. "Should we load it on one of the trucks to take with us?"

"There's a burn spot out back by the trash barrels," Sherri offered. "You can just pile it all back there for now and burn it later." She turned back to Dylan. "Y'all can still burn garbage out here in the country, can't you? I've lived in the city for a long time." She gave Dylan a warm smile.

"I think we're far enough out of town for that, but a big fire might draw attention coming from this hill," he said, returning her smile. "Show me where and, Jeremy, you guys can just carry it all out there as you take it off. One of you can tell Jake to do the same with the siding."

"Sure, boss," the young man said and nodded at Sherri.

Sherri led him out the back door and across the lawn to a spot where two rusty fifty-gallon barrels stood up on blackened concrete blocks. The green sprouts of fresh weeds poked up through burned off grass and wild plants.

"This is where my grandpa burned garbage and stuff," she said and waved her arm toward the barrels and burned off spot. "If it's going to be a big pile, we may need to mow off some of those taller weeds, so we don't set the whole field on fire, though."

"Good idea," he said and stared off across the field where tall, brown rye grass waved in the soft Autumn breeze. "With the carpet, the siding, and the paneling, it could be a pretty big and pretty hot fire. I'll have a couple of the guys come out here with a weed whacker and cut it all back five or six feet just to be safe and maybe dig a little trench as a fire break."

"That tall, dry grass catches fast in the Fall when it's dry like this," she said as she enjoyed the warm sun on her face and the cool breeze in her hair.

"Granny was burning something out here once and let it get away from her," Sherri began, but her breath caught in her throat with emotion as she thought about her grandmother and she pretended to cough as a tear slipped from her eye to slide down her cheek. She turned from Dylan and brushed it away.

He saw it, though, and put an arm around her shoulder and pulled her close. "You miss them, huh? I read about their accident in the paper. I'm so sorry," he said softly into her hair.

Damn, this isn't gonna be pretty. Why did I have to think about Granny?

"Yah," Sherri said and turned her head into his shoulder. "They were all I really ever had." His man-scent overwhelmed her for a moment and Sherri melted into him with a muffled sob. He put his other arm around her and stood holding her as she allowed herself to grieve again for her lost grandparents.

Now I'm acting like a blubbering idiot, but it feels good to have a man's arms around me. It's been too damned long.

Sherri stepped back reluctantly after a few minutes and gazed up into his sympathetic brown eyes, embarrassed at her emotional display. "I'm sorry," she sniffed and wiped her eyes. with the back of her hand.

"It's all right," he said and reached into his pocket for a handkerchief. "Here," he said and handed it to her.

Sherri took the white piece of linen, wiped her eyes, and blew her nose. She stuffed it into her pocket and grinned. "I'll wash that and give it back tomorrow."

"No hurry," he assured her with a worried smile, "I have a drawer full of them at home anyway. Don't worry about it." He waved his hand, dismissing the subject of his handkerchief.

"I have to do a load of laundry today, anyhow."

"Hey," he said and touched Sherri's shoulder, "want to go with me to that thing at the Besty-Westy on Saturday night?"

Sherri's eyes went wide and her mouth fell open in surprise.

Is Dylan Roberts actually asking me out on a freakin' date? I'm out here ballin' my freakin' eyes out and snotting up his handkerchief and he's asking me out? It's probably just a mercy date. He's probably feeling sorry for me.

"I thought that thing was last Saturday," Sherri said and sniffed.

"There was some flu going around or something," he said and shrugged his shoulders. "It got rescheduled to this weekend." He took a deep breath. "So, do ya want to go?"

"I don't know, Dylan," Sherri sighed, "I was never a part of your crowd in school. I'd feel out of place and uncomfortable with those people."

"Oh, come on," he pled, "I hate going to the damned things alone. I'm usually the only single guy there." He took her hand. "It'll be a blast. The food's pretty good, and I'm sure everyone will be thrilled to see you after all this time."

I can't believe he's holding my hand. Dylan freaking Roberts is holding my hand.

Sherri rolled her eyes. "I don't know about that. Candi's going to be there, isn't she? I'm sure she has them all ready to string me up over Lost Hope."

"I think you can hold your own against Candi Clem any day, Sherri," he said and chuckled deep in his throat. "What about it? Be my date?" He squeezed her hand and smiled warmly. "We can talk about the house and I can write it off as a business dinner. Bobby will like that. What do you say?"

"Oh, all right," she relented, "We'll talk about burning the trash so Bobby can write it off as a business expense."

"Or we could talk about book ideas and *you* could write it off," he said and grinned.

"You mean you're asking me out, but I have to pay for my own meal?" she said with a sheepish grin.

He stared at her for a minute, but then broke into a grin. "I forgot how you could always make me laugh, Sherri." He put one of his big hands on her shoulder and squeezed. "I think I've been missing that in my life for a while now. I always enjoyed talking to you. You were so funny."

Sherri furrowed her brow in confusion. His touch felt nice and being in his arms had been amazing.

Now what the hell is he talking about? I don't recall us ever talking that much. Don't read anything into this, Lambert.

"Someone to make me laugh," he said and surprised Sherri by taking her hand in his. "You always made me laugh with your little side-comments in English class.

Is he really holding my hand again? I feel like a damned teenager.

"Oh," she sighed and took a deep breath. "OK, I'll go with you and be the comic relief for the evening." Sherri smiled and wiped her eyes again.

This should be interesting.

"Thanks," he said and squeezed her hand again. "You're a life saver. I really do hate going to those things alone."

As they turned back toward the house, the six men on his crew scattered back into the house from the back porch where they'd been watching their boss with the owner of their project house in his arms.

Well, that shouldn't take long to get around town. Men are bigger gossips than women any day.

❦ 7 ❦

Sherri bolted up in her bed. Someone was playing ragtime music on her grandmother's old upright piano. As she slid out of the bed, Sherri glanced at the red numbers glowing on the clock by her bed. They read three-fifteen. She smelled cigarette smoke and frowned.

Who the hell is smoking in my damned house?

Sherri didn't allow anyone to smoke in the house. Cigarette smoking was one of her pet peeves. It irritated her sinuses and gave her a headache. She'd been firm with the work crew about not smoking in the house and knew some of them had been upset about having to go outside to light up.

She crept to the door and peeked out into the living room. At the piano sat the blonde girl from her dreams. Her short blonde curls bounced as her hands danced over the keys of the old piano and the fringe and glass beads on her blue, flapper-era dress shimmered in the light cast by the flames in the fireplace.

Is this another dream? Why have they become so realistic lately? They were never like this before.

Two other women stood on either side of the upright piano with glasses in their hands. Another glass filled with clear liquid sat on the top of the piano beside a heavy glass ashtray. The smoke from three unfiltered cigarettes spiraled up toward the ceiling. At first, Sherri thought the glass held water, but the slices of lime floating in them told Sherri the glass held gin instead.

Great, cigarettes and booze. What's going on here?

Sherri glanced around and recognized her living room, but like the bedroom in her dreams, it looked subtly different. The paneling was gone, and the fireplace had been uncovered. A heavy, dark wood mantle that looked to Sherri like a railroad tie was mounted above the flames in the hearth. Above the mantle, a taxidermy deer stared out into the room with brown, glass eyes.

Blue wallpaper with vertical stripes of pink vining flowers covered the plastered walls. Lacy curtains hung at the windows with metal Venetian blinds beneath them. Rag rugs littered the polished wooden floors in place of the dingy gold carpet.

It's the same, but different like my bedroom was.

Her furniture had disappeared or changed, as well. Her green, suede sofa and love seat had been replaced with a bulky leather couch with metal arms and a matching chair and ottoman. Sturdy wood tables stood beside the couch and chair with hurricane lamps and glass ashtrays atop them. Her flat-screen television was gone, as well as her laptop. Her grandmother's piano looked different, too. Its finish was bright and glossy rather than cracked and bubbled with age.

What is going on here? Is this another damned dream? What did I eat before going to bed? Maybe I should ask for some sleeping pills.

"What the hell," Sherri swore as she grabbed onto the door frame for support. Her heart beat like a drum in her chest, her head had begun to spin, and she thought she might pass out at any minute. The room was cold.

What in heaven's name is going on here? I know I'm not dreaming this. I'm completely awake and I feel like I'm gonna throw up.

The music suddenly stopped, and the three women turned to stare at Sherri. "Oh, hi, Doll," the blonde said cheerfully. "Did we wake ya? That's never happened before." The blonde's brow furrowed in confusion.

At least I'm not the only one who thinks this is weird.

"Who are you?" Sherri stammered. "And what are you doing in my house?"

The girl let out a drunken cackle and slapped one of the other women's arms. "She thinks this is *her* house." The girl grabbed her glass off the piano, turned back to Sherri, and said, "Doll, this has been *our* house for a damned sight longer than you've been around." She tipped up the glass and took a long swallow.

"But who are you, though?" Sherri asked again. "And why are you here?"

"I'm Molly," the girl said, "and these dolls are Tillie and Maudie." The other women, who appeared to be a decade older and a few pounds heavier than Molly, nodded to Sherri and smiled. "Like I said before, we've been here for a long time … too long, for a fact."

She looked up at the two women then reached for one of the cigarettes, put it to her perfect little pink mouth, inhaled, and then blew out a stream of blue smoke into the room.

"I'm sorry, but I don't allow smoking in my … eh … the house," Sherri stammered uneasily. "It gives me a splitting headache."

"Oh, sorry, Doll," Molly said and stubbed out her cigarette. "Girls, why don't you gals take the smokes outside while I have a little chat with the doll, here."

The room shimmered and the two women disappeared along with the ashtray and the cigarettes. Sherri grabbed at the door for support as she grew dizzy.

This is all too damned weird.

She glanced out the window and saw the tiny red, glowing dots of the cigarettes on the porch outside as though the women had moved to the swing on the porch. She felt nauseous and thought she was going to throw up but swallowed hard and remained on her feet.

"Now what are all y'all doing in my house?" Sherri asked the girl sitting at the piano again. "And what's with all the noise tonight?"

"There ya go again with that *my house* bullshit, Doll," Molly sighed and stretched her petite, lean body. "I've been tryin' to explain it to ya. Me and the gals have been here for a very long time. We need ya to find what's left of us and give us a proper send off with a preacher sayin' words over us and all.

"I'm sorry we woke ya with our little party, but we gotta pass the time somehow," she said with a pout and shrugged her petite shoulders. "Waitin' to move to the other side is tiresome."

Oh, my god, they're ghosts. My freaking house is haunted by a bunch of flappers!

"Weren't you given a funeral before you were buried?" Sherri asked, but suddenly felt silly, talking to a ghost as though it were a living person.

"Oh," Molly snorted and took another sip from the tall glass, "we were buried all right, but we never got no proper words said over us to send us on our way. Without the words said by a proper preacher man, we're bound here and can't join our families. That's why we need ya to find us, Doll. We got people waitin' for us on the other side and they can't go to their rest 'til they've seen us across."

That's a concept I've never considered before. Spirits need to be released from the earthly plain by a holy man before they can cross to wherever. Makes sense, I suppose. All religions have funeral rites for the dead.

"I don't know how I can help, though," Sherri said and shrugged her shoulders.

"Oh, you and that man of yours will peel back the years and figure it all out," Molly said, but her face darkened before she added, "Watch out for that man, though, Doll. He's got bad blood runnin' through his veins, really bad blood."

What man of mine? I don't have a damned man.

Sherri frowned. "What do you mean by that?"

All Molly said before she faded away was, "I've tried to show you for years now, Doll. Look closer the next time and you'll see what I mean."

Look closer at what?

The room shimmered and Sherri squeezed her eyes shut. When she opened them again, the room had returned to normal with the white light glowing on her laptop where it rested on the arm of her sofa, charging. The irritating smell of cigarettes had disappeared from the room along with the women.

I guess we still get to enjoy our vices in the afterlife. Good to know.

A violent wave of nausea hit Sherri. She slapped a hand over her mouth and ran to the bathroom where she dropped to her knees and violently emptied her stomach into the pink toilet. She heaved until nothing but air came up. Her abdomen ached from the retching, and Sherri knew she would be sore across her middle tomorrow.

This can't be happening. Maybe it's stress from all the activity with the renovation or worry over writing the new books. Maybe I'm just stressing over the damned date with Dylan.

She rested her head on the cool porcelain for a few minutes before pulling herself to her feet. Sherri rinsed her mouth with some cold water from the faucet, wiped her sweaty face, and stumbled back through the cold, empty house toward the dark bedroom.

She crawled back between the sheets as the red numbers on her clock turned over to four-twenty-five.

I know I wasn't dreaming this time. I was wide awake and standing in the damned living room for an hour. I wasn't dreaming about Molly this time. I was standing in there talking to her. That's never happened before.

Sherri tossed and turned for an hour, running the strange conversation she'd had with Molly's ghost through her head. She was certain the women had been ghosts. Molly said they needed to be found and given proper burials.

She said she'd been trying to show me something for years. Does that mean they were never dreams, after all? Has Molly been sending me visions since I was a kid, trying to show me something to help her and those other women?

What did she think a damned kid could do to help them back then? Hell, what does she think an old woman like me can do for them now? And why me, for god's sake? This is all too weird.

❧ 8 ❧

Due to her very early morning visit, Sherri slept until almost eleven. At least it was Saturday and the workmen hadn't been there to wake her before seven.

She dragged herself from bed, stiff and sore, with her head pounding. She stopped in the kitchen long enough to put on a pot of coffee and then made her way into the bathroom to turn on the shower.

I need hot water to clear my head and then coffee.

She stood beneath the spray of hot water until it began to run cooler, ignoring her phone when it chimed with a text.

It's the damned weekend. Whoever it is can wait until I'm done.

Sherri stepped out of the tub onto the rough floor. The mosaic of black and pink tiles had been carefully taken up a few days before in preparation for the new. She dried her body, wrapped her dripping red curls in the towel, and slipped into her robe before following her nose into the kitchen where life-saving hot coffee awaited.

She sat down at the table with her cup of coffee

and picked up her phone. Sherri smiled when she saw the text was from Dylan.

RR: I'll pick you up at six. Dress casual.

Sherri frowned, bent, and began pounding her forehead on the table. She'd very nearly forgotten her promise to accompany Dylan to the dinner at the Best Western that night.

Why the hell didn't I go with my gut and stick with my original 'no'? This is going to be a fucking disaster. Candi is gonna be there and cause a scene. I just know it. I should have said no.

She reflected with a frown that her high school experience might have benefitted from her having said 'no' more often.

Hindsight is better than foresight, Lambert, so just get over it. What's done is done.

After an hour and two cups of strong, black coffee, Sherri's headache had begun to fade. She rose reluctantly from the table and took the towel from her head to shake out her damp curls.

Before entering the living room, Sherri tentatively stuck her head through the door to make certain she was walking into the living room she knew and not one from the alternate reality she'd experienced earlier that morning.

It was *her* living room. Relieved, Sherri sped through the room and into her bedroom. She made her bed and tidied up the room before going to her closet where she stood holding the door open as she peered in the way a teenage boy stands with the refrigerator door open, staring in search of an elusive snack. She had no idea what she was going to wear to this thing tonight.

Dress casual my ass. Neither Candi nor Kitty are going to be dressed better than me tonight. Those days are done.

৩%চ

Sherri spent the afternoon on her laptop. She enjoyed the work and it took her mind off the upcoming evening and what it might have in store.

Dylan's eyes went wide and his mouth dropped open when Sherri opened the door that evening and he mouthed, "Wow."

He bent to kiss her as she let him in the door, and she offered her cheek rather than her lips.

Don't get ahead of yourself, big guy. Let's see where this night goes.

Sherri had finally settled on a brown leather skirt that fit tight and fell well above her knees, but below the tops of her thigh-high stockings. With that she wore a cashmere, cowl-neck sweater, and a form-fitting tweed jacket with patches on the elbows in the same shade of tan suede as her spike-heeled boots. She finished the ensemble with her Rolex, diamond-stud earrings, and a diamond and ruby cocktail ring.

Let's see you bitches top this.

Sherri had brushed her hair up into a smooth chignon and pinned it with diamond-studded hairpins—well, not mined diamonds, but lab manufactured. They sparkled the same and only a gemologist would be able to tell the difference.

Her makeup was perfect with an airbrushed foundation and dark smoky eyes, the slightest blush of pink tinted her cheeks, and frosty pink her lips. She'd manicured her nails and applied the same shade of pink as on her lips.

"You look great," Dylan said as she stepped back

and did a quick twirl so he could get a good look at the complete outfit.

"It's not too much, is it?" she asked, not caring if he thought it was.

"Not at all," he said. "My daughter, the fashionista, would call it casual elegance and it looks perfect."

"Thanks," Sherri said, and she could feel his eyes on her ass in the tight skirt as she bent over the coffee table to grab her purse that matched the brown suede boots. She turned back to him and smiled. "I guess I'm ready then." She followed him out the door, turned, and locked it.

I'm crazy, but I guess I'm doing this.

Dylan took her by the arm and walked with her to a late model, silver BMW. He opened the passenger door and Sherri got in.

"Nice ride," she said as she settled herself into the comfortable burgundy leather seat.

"Company car," he said with a wink and closed the door. Sherri watched him walk around the front of the car and then drop in behind the wheel. He turned to her and said with a smile, "You really do look beautiful tonight."

"You look pretty dapper yourself," she said and returned his smile.

Dylan wore creased, blue jeans and a light-blue, striped oxford shirt with a white button-down collar and a braided leather bolo tie. The light color of the shirt accentuated his tanned skin and dark eyes.

I think he's hotter now than when we were in school. Maturity looks good on him.

The heels on his polished cowboy boots added to his height and Sherri was glad she'd worn hers. If she'd worn flats, he'd have been nearly a foot taller than her.

She stared at him in the fading light from outside and smiled. He looked more like an aging cowboy tonight, than a Mafioso, though the BMW spoke more to New York than New Mexico.

I thought I left all the cowboy wannabes in California, but it looks good on him.

"Who's going to be there tonight," Sherri asked uneasily, thinking of Candi.

"There will probably be a pretty big crowd tonight," he said as he backed out of the driveway. "It's Louis' birthday this month too and he'll be there with his crowd." He winked and gave her an impish grin. "Our crowd isn't quite as tame as his, though."

"I don't know about that," Sherri said and chuckled. "Didn't he and Jim Myers let loose all the fruit flies from the biology lab into the cafeteria our sophomore year?"

"Oh, yah, I forgot about that," Dylan said with a laugh. "I don't think they're quite that wild anymore, though. Louis works at the library and Jim's an accountant.

"Both guys are married with kids and grandkids now," he said with a sad smile, "and their buddy Kevin died of a heart attack a few years back. "Remember how everyone used to call them the alphabet—J, K, & L?"

"Well, not everyone," Sherri said. "I think that was just a snot-squad thing."

"Oh, yah," he said, and his smile faded at the mention of what others in school called his clique.

They drove the few miles in silence until they turned into the Best Western's asphalt parking lot.

"Looks pretty full," Sherri said hesitantly.

"About the only place to go on a Saturday night in Barrett," Dylan said as he found a parking spot in the back. "Unless you want to go to The Limits or The Downtowner." He glanced at her outfit again and smiled. "You're way overdressed for either of those dumps."

"There's an Applebee's in town now," she said cheerfully and waved toward the far side of the highway where the new restaurant had been built.

"And it's always packed on the weekends," he snorted as he got out of the car.

Dylan opened her door and took her hand as they walked through the crowded parking lot and into the Best Western. They passed the front desk, walked through the busy dining room, and into a private dining room set with six round tables and eight chairs at each table.

All the tables were full except the farthest one from the door. The room went noticeably quieter as she and Dylan entered and walked toward the empty table. Sherri saw Candi lean to the woman sitting beside her and whisper something as they passed.

This is going to be a fucking disaster. Maybe it's not too late to say I have the cramps or started my period or something.

Dylan was holding Sherri's chair as she sat, when Candi came marching over to their table.

And it begins.

"I had my mother read that book of yours, Sherri," Candi stormed, "and she's gonna write that publisher of yours and tell them she's suing for slander if they don't take every book off the shelves."

"Oh, really?" Sherri said and stood. She smiled at Candi as she very slowly took off her jacket to reveal her heavy breasts and narrow waist in the tight sweater. She turned her back to Candi, bent to show her shapely ass in the tight leather skirt and draped the jacket over the back of the chair.

Get a load of that, you big-mouth, fat cow. Maybe you should try some of your husband's product. I hear meth is great for weight loss.

"It's only slander if it is untruthful," Sherri continued as she sat again.

"Defamation of character, then," Candi snarled. "You defamed me, my family, and this whole town, Sherri." She bent over the table and narrowed her eyes at Sherri. "I'm gonna tell everybody in town to buy that damned book and then sue your ass."

Sherri turned to Dylan and said loudly, "Six thousand or so sales should make my publisher very happy." She raised her hand and rubbed her first three fingers with her thumb—the international symbol for money.

"You're a bitch, Sherri and we're gonna get you for it," Candi snarled with her cheeks red.

"Candi," Sherri asked in a sugary-sweet voice, "Have you ever read that little legal paragraph on the title page of most books that says the book is a work of *fiction* and any resemblance to people or places is a coincidence and the product of the author's imagination?"

Sherri took a sip of the ice water the waitress had just set in front of her. "That little paragraph keeps the publisher and author from being liable from frivolous lawsuits."

"Sit down, Candi," Dylan said in a commanding voice. "You're making a damned fool of yourself."

"*I'm* making a fool of *myself?*" Candi snarled at Dylan. "I can't believe you brought *her* here to our party. You're the one who looks like a damned fool, Dylan. She's had half the guys in this room between her legs."

"And you've had the other half," Dylan shot back.

"More like three quarters," another male voice said, and Candi whipped her head around to glare at her husband who stood, putting on his jacket.

"I ain't never been between your pretty lady's legs, Dylan," Terry Clem said as Candi stomped past. She glared at him as she moved toward the door.

"I ain't been between hers in a damned long time, neither," he yelled after Candi as she stormed out to the twittering laughter of people at the tables.

"And don't guess I will be for a damned sight longer now," he said sadly as he bent to pick up Candi's purse. He waved. "See y'all next month ... if she hasn't slit my throat."

Sherri watched the aging drug dealer leave and she turned as Dylan took her hand. "I'm so sorry, Dylan. I shouldn't have come. I'm sorry if I've embarrassed you in front of your friends."

"Are you kidding me?" he said with a broad smile and squeezed her hand. "Look around at everyone. This is the most excitement we've had at one of these things ... ever." He gave her a broad grin.

"And it was at fucking Candi's expense. I told you that you could hold your own against her any day." He reached over and kissed Sherri's cheek. "You're smarter than she is and always were. It's what she hated about you."

"I suppose," Sherri sighed and took another sip of water as she stared around the room of smiling faces. "I just hate fucking confrontation."

Maybe I'll be able to get through this thing now that Candi is gone.

They ordered steaks, loaded baked potatoes, and salads. Sherri asked for a Jack and Coke after Dylan ordered a Canadian Club on the rocks. She drank the whisky drink while they waited for their food to arrive and then she asked for a glass of sweet red wine to have with her food.

As they were finishing their piece of birthday cake, Louis walked up, wearing a brightly colored, cone-shaped birthday hat on his gray head.

"Hi, Sherri," he said with a broad grin, "did you read that book I suggested about Miles Tucker and his crime spree here in the area?"

"I did," she said and emptied her wine glass. "But I still have some questions."

"About Tucker or your property?" He asked and shifted his eyes to Dylan as her date stood.

"I need another drink," Dylan said, shoved his chair under the table, and strode away without saying any more.

Did I do something? Surely, he's not embarrassed for Louis to see us together.

"I wonder what's with him?" Sherri said as she watched Dylan leave the room.

"He hasn't told you, then," Louis said and pushed his thick glasses up on the bridge of his nose.

He's certainly never mentioned Miles Tucker.

"Told me what?" Sherri asked as her eyes flitted toward the door Dylan had walked through.

"Miles Tucker was Dylan's great uncle on his mother's side," Louis said uneasily. "Tucker was his mother's maiden name and Miles was her uncle."

No, he certainly never mentioned anything, not even when he saw me reading that book. I wonder why. Tucker's been dead for decades.

Louis glanced around the room. "Miles Tucker is the skeleton in the family closet. Her brothers even went as far as to change their names legally from Tucker to Stuckey out of embarrassment and nobody admits to being related."

"Oh, my," Sherri sighed. "I wonder why he never

told me. Working on my house must be terrible for him. Why did he even take the job?"

"Probably thought he had to," Louis said and then leaned in closer to Sherri. "I heard that Bobby had made some … eh … bad investments," he stammered, "and the company is in trouble."

"Oh, my," she said again. "I hope it's going to remain solvent. I just wrote them a big check to finish the renovation of my house."

"I wouldn't worry about that, Sherri," Louis said and patted her hand. "I've known Dylan Roberts since we were in grade school and he's probably one of the most responsible people I know. He'll make sure your house gets finished … even if he has to pay for and do it himself." He patted Sherri hand again. "Now, what else was it you were wanting to know about Tucker?"

Sherri glanced back toward the door but didn't see Dylan. "You said something before about missing women and Tucker. Didn't you?" She asked and shrugged her shoulders. "There wasn't anything at all in the book about any missing women and Miles Tucker. It just talked about his bootlegging and the murders of the men he was tried and hanged for."

"I'm not surprised," Louis said with a long sigh. "Back then women who'd have associated with a gangster like Tucker would have been considered trash. The police probably just shrugged their shoulders, said good riddance to bad rubbish, and forgot all about them."

"Things sure have changed, haven't they?" Sherri sighed. "Young celebrity girls these days search out gang-bangers to club with. I bet if one of them went missing, the cops would look under every rock until they were found."

"I'm sure you're right, but those girls who went

missing in Tucker's time were just country girls or from working class families." Louis rolled his eyes behind his thick glasses. "I'm sure that if they'd come from Jasper county's upper-crust families, more attention would have been paid to their disappearances, but they weren't."

"Then things haven't changed so much around Barrett, then," Sherri said sarcastically. "Those of us from the country are still looked down upon as second class."

"You're probably right, I'm afraid." He glanced toward his table of friends. "I'd better be getting back," he said and stood, "but I'll put my researcher hat on next week and see what I can find in the Microfiche from back then. There might have been something in the papers about the disappearances."

"Thanks, Louis," she said as he started back to his table. "And Happy Birthday."

As Sherri waited for Dylan to return, Connie Harris from the Barrett News approached her about doing an interview for the paper's Sunday supplement and Jill Tennant, who had opened a small coffee shop and book store, asked Sherri about getting some of her books for her store as well as the possibility of her coming to do a signing and speak to a writing group that met there on a weekly basis.

"You see," Dylan said after Jill left their table. "I told you everybody would be glad to see you."

"Oh," Sherri scoffed, "I've written a few books and they think they're rubbing shoulders with a celebrity or something." Sherri picked up the drink he'd brought her from the bar and took a long swallow. "It's no big deal."

"It *is* a big deal, Sherri," he said and smiled warmly. "And after the way you handled Candi in front of everyone, you *are* a celebrity."

He wrapped his arm around her shoulder and pulled her close. Sherri turned her face up and their lips met. At first it was a soft kiss, but after Sherri opened her mouth and allowed him to push his tongue past her teeth, it became something more.

Is he really kissing me here in front of everybody?

Dylan brought his hand to the back of her head and crushed her mouth to his. She, in turn, wrapped her arms around him and ran her fingers through his hair and gently scratched his scalp.

This is nice, but it might just be a result of all the Canadian Club.

A thrill ran through Sherri from her nipples to her clit. Everything began to throb as their tongues twined around one another's and her heart began to flutter in her chest. She tasted the rich caramel of the aged whisky in his mouth, but it wasn't unpleasant.

It's been too damned long since I've had a man between my legs.

Sherri broke away from Dylan when she noticed the room had grown quiet. When she opened her eyes, people at the other tables quickly averted theirs and Sherri felt her cheeks flush with embarrassment.

"Did we just get caught necking in the library?" Dylan asked with a soft chuckle and brushed her cheek with one of his fingers.

Sherri gazed up into his big brown eyes, fringed with thick dark lashes. He was still the hottest guy in their class. "Something like that, I think," she whispered with a smile on her lips.

I can't believe I'm on a date with Dylan Roberts and everyone knows.

"Wanna get out of here?" he asked and used his thumb to wipe some smudged lipstick from her upper lip.

"Please," she pled and rolled her eyes.

Dylan held her chair as she stood and helped her on with her jacket. He bent and whispered into her ear from behind as she buttoned her jacket, "You were the most beautiful woman here tonight, Sherri, and I'm proud to call you my date."

Oh, my goodness. He's so sweet. I can't believe he just said that. Maybe he hasn't been between anybody's legs in a while and is trying to get on my good side. I think he's there.

He took her hand and they walked toward the door.

"Hey, Dylan, tap that once for me tonight, will ya," a male voice called as they passed the table where Candi and her husband had been sitting. A female voice was quick to chide, but the voice continued. "It was pretty tight as I recall and she could go over and over all night long, squealing like a little pig with every stroke."

Dylan squeezed her hand, glanced down, and said, "Don't let Alan Parker get to you. He's a fucking loud-mouth drunk."

"I know," Sherri sighed, "but I never even fucked him."

"I know that and so does everyone else," Dylan said and brought her hand to his full, warm lips. "Alan is a legend in his own mind."

He was an ass in school and he's still an ass. Why can't some people ever grow up?

They left the building and the cool, moist air was a welcome relief to Sherri when it hit her face. Dylan continued to hold her hand as they walked to the car.

This feels so nice. I haven't been on a date in a long time.

"I think we're in for rain," Dylan said and pointed up at the heavy clouds obscuring the moon.

"I suppose I'd better be getting home before my coach turns into a pumpkin," Sherri said and grinned into the cloudy night.

"It had better not," Dylan said as he opened the door and she slid into the cold interior. "If I took the Beamer back orange, Bobby would have a fucking cow."

❧ 9 ❧

Dylan took his time as he drove back to Sherri's with the radio turned up loud on the Classic Rock station. Fat raindrops began to splat on the windshield as they passed the little bar at the edge of Barrett called The Limits and Dylan switched on the wipers.

They laughed when they compared stories about something that had happened to each of them when they'd first heard a particular song playing.

Damn, she can make me laugh like a kid again with her funny stories.

When Dylan pulled into her drive, he switched off the wipers, killed the engine, scooted over in his seat, and reached across to pull Sherri close. The console between the seats made it difficult, but he had to have another kiss and maybe if he was lucky, a little more from the pretty woman.

I may not have gotten a piece of her in high school, but I have her here tonight. She certainly turns me on.

Their kiss in the restaurant had ignited something in Dylan he hadn't felt with a woman in a long time. He wanted her more right now than he'd wanted a woman in longer than he could remember.

If he played his cards right maybe she'd give him a little tonight. He pulled Sherri close and kissed her again.

The thought of crawling between those shapely, long legs made his dick begin to swell in his jeans. Dylan found the hem of her sweater and slid his hand inside to touch her hot, smooth skin. Sherri didn't pull away and Dylan took that as an invitation to continue.

She always had the greatest looking tits.

He came to her breast and slid his fingers into her bra until he found a hard nipple. Sherri sighed as he pinched and twisted the solid little mound of flesh and he wished he had it in his mouth.

My fucking dick is going to explode in a minute. I wonder…

He slid his free hand over and up her stockinged legs and came to the top of her thigh-high hose. He continued along the inside of her thigh until he felt warm flesh. Soon he felt coarse hair, wet with her juices and he stopped.

She's not wearing underwear! That's so fucking hot. Thigh-highs and no panties. That's like the best porn dream ever.

Dylan pushed his hand farther until his fingers were tangled in the damp hair between Sherri's legs. He kissed her harder and rolled the nipple between his thumb and forefinger. She whimpered and moaned with pleasure.

His finger pushed into her pussy and it was wet. Before he slid inside her completely, he found her clit and massaged it gently. Sherri's tensed legs relaxed, and Dylan slid his finger in and out of her hot, wet pussy.

Oh, my god. She's so hot and wet. I wonder if I can make her cum with just my fingers.

Sherri's attitude bolstered his confidence and emboldened Dylan. He pushed up Sherri's soft sweater, tugged down her bra, releasing her beautiful breasts.

He bent uncomfortably over the console to pull her hard nipple between his teeth and suck with his tongue flicking over the hard knot playfully. Dylan slid his finger in and out of her in a slow, steady rhythm, careful to put pressure on her swollen clit as he passed over it. Sherri gasped and moaned every time he did.

I want to fuck her so bad. I want to feel that pussy wrapped around my dick and I want to shoot her full of cum.

Sherri continued to sigh and moan with his attention to her hard nipples and her swollen clit. He grabbed her hand and brought it over to rest on his jeans over his throbbing erection. He deftly unbuckled his belt, popped the button, unzipped his jeans, and pulled out his hard dick.

I don't know if I can make her cum, but all she's gonna have to do is stroke it a couple of times to make me blow my wad all over the damned car.

"This is nice," Sherri whispered and began to stroke his erection with her warm, soft fingers. "I can't wait to feel it inside me, Dylan."

Dylan moaned into her breast as she ran her nails gently over his hard, throbbing dick. He bit her nipple harder than he intended and Sherri yelped.

"I'm sorry," he mumbled as he gently kissed the wet nipple.

"It's all right," she sighed and began to pump her hips to meet his thrusting finger.

Oh, my God, that's so hot.

Dylan released his seat and let it slide all the way back. He took hold of her hips and with all his strength, lifted Sherri up out of her seat and over the console. She pushed her skirt up over her hips and somehow managed to get her right leg past the steering wheel to straddle Dylan's lap and his erect penis.

They both moaned as she slid down onto his throbbing dick. His rough zipper dug into his tender flesh as Sherri settled all the way down on his dick.

That feels so damned good.

"Fuck me good, baby," he moaned. "I really need it."

Damn, she's tight, but she's so fucking wet.

"Me too," she sighed and threw back her head. "It's been too damned long."

Dylan reached around her and adjusted the steering wheel, so she had more room and Sherri began to use her hands on his shoulders to lift her hips and slide her hot pussy up and down on his throbbing dick.

Damn, she does that nice and her tits are fantastic.

He caught one of her bouncing nipples in his mouth and sucked, causing Sherri to gasp and tighten the muscles in her pussy around his throbbing dick.

Fuck, no woman's ever done that to my dick before. This is all so hot; fucking her in my car in her damned driveway. We're like a couple of kids on a Saturday night. Damn, I'm gonna cum.

"I'm gonna cum baby," he gasped. "I can't hold it much longer."

Sherri moaned and picked up her pace, "Yah, me too." She dug her nails into his shoulders and Dylan felt her body tense. "Oh, god," she groaned, and Dylan felt her pussy tighten around his dick again and then begin to pulse. "Yaaahh," she moaned with her release.

This is so fucking hot. I've never experienced anything like it. Never

Her tight, pulsing pussy, along with her groan, excited Dylan, and he tightened his grip on her hips and arched up into her as his cum blasted out into her. "Jeez, yes," he groaned and threw back his head on the seat. "Fuck, yah that's great."

Dylan wrapped his arms around Sherri's body, ignoring her disheveled clothes that were bunched up around her waist, and pulled her close. He rested his face between her heaving breasts and felt her heart pounding beneath his cheeks. He wanted to laugh, and he wanted to cry.

I haven't had this much fun with a woman in longer than I can remember.

Sherri pushed back and rested her back against the steering wheel. She stared down into his face and grinned. "This probably would have been a lot more comfortable inside in my bed."

"No," he said and squeezed one of her ass cheeks, "this was absolutely perfect." He let out a long sigh. "If I'd known you were such a good fuck, I'd have given you a go back in school."

The grin faded from Sherri's face and anger flashed in her green eyes. She rolled off his lap and back into the passenger's seat. She tugged her sweater down over her breasts and pulled at her skirt.

Oh, shit. What a moron I am. That didn't come out right at all.

Sherri grabbed her purse from the floorboard, shoved open the door and, pulling at her jumbled clothes, jumped out of the car into the pouring rain.

"I'm sorry, Sherri," he called to her, "that came out all wrong."

"Yah, it did," she snarled and slammed the door in his face.

Fuck! I'm such an idiot. Should I go after her and try to explain what I meant?

On the porch, Sherri fumbled with the key to open the door. Dylan opened the car door, but as he was about to step out into the rain, she slammed the door and turned off the porch light.

Probably a good indicator that she doesn't want to see my face again tonight … if ever. I'm such a fucking moron.

❦ 10 ❦

Sherri stormed to the house with the cold rain flattening her disheveled hair, and Dylan's warm semen running down her thighs.

That son-of-a-bitch hasn't changed at all. He's still the same damned prick he was in school.

She wiped frustrated tears along with raindrops from her eyes as she fumbled to find the keyhole. As Sherri unlocked the door, she heard Dylan's door open behind her. She hurried inside, slammed the door, and flipped off the porch light.

I am so done with men. I'm just gonna get this house project finished and concentrate on my writing. The men in my books are the only ones I need in my life now.

Inside the house, Sherri dashed more tears from her eyes as she dropped her purse onto the loveseat and shrugged out of her wet jacket. She stomped into the bathroom, tugging her sweater off over her head as she went. She pitched it in the corner and dropped onto the toilet to unzip her wet, suede boots.

Sherri peeled off her hose and tossed them along with their garter onto the floor with the sweater. More tears ran down her cheeks as she wiped Dylan's semen from her inner thighs.

How could I have been so stupid to think the entitled asshole had actually changed into a decent human being?

Sherri stood in front of the mirror and stared at her mascara-streaked face. She pulled the pins from her hair and shook it out. Her limp, red curls cascaded down around her face and Sherri pushed them aside to take out her earrings. She dropped them on the sink and then unfastened her watch and draped the band beside the diamond studs.

What a horrible night. How could I have been such a fool?

Sherri turned on the shower, waited for the water to heat, and then stepped beneath the hot spray. She turned her face up to allow the water to wash away what remained of her carefully applied make up.

What a waste. I should have stayed at home with my laptop and been productive. All I managed to accomplish tonight, was to add to my already bad reputation.

Disgusted with herself, Sherri took the washrag and scrubbed between her legs, as if scrubbing away his semen would scrub Dylan Roberts from her heart and mind.

Much too upset to sleep after her shower, Sherri plopped onto the couch and opened her laptop. As it neared midnight, Sherri had managed to write two more chapters and kill off two minor male characters in gruesome manners.

I really shouldn't write when I'm pissed.

She smiled wickedly as she closed her laptop and set it aside to trudge into the bedroom and crawl between the sheets. Her eyes throbbed from crying and her vagina throbbed from the workout it had gotten with Dylan.

I hate that I enjoyed it so much.

Sherri woke late the next morning. She got up and staggered into the kitchen where she started a pot of strong coffee. She intended to spend the day writing.

It would be quiet without the work crew knocking around the house and she hoped to get several thousand words in before the end of the day. Sherri also hoped it would keep her mind from going back to Dylan and the night before.

I just want to sit here, go into a world of my own, and forget last night for a little while.

She took her coffee and her charged-up laptop out to the porch, where the morning sun sparkled on the wet grass. The Fall morning was warm, causing mists to rise off the fields around her property. As she sipped her coffee, Sherri enjoyed the beautiful, peaceful morning.

Maroon and gold mums bloomed in the beds around the yard and the grass hadn't yet turned from green to brown. Leaves on the oaks and hickories in the nearby stand of woods were turning yellow and red. They would soon be falling to the forest floor as November approached.

Sherri saw a corn picker in a field across the valley. Last night's rain must have hurried the farmer into his field on this Sunday morning in fear of more before he could get his crop in.

Her phone kept chiming with texts, and she suspected they were from Dylan. She ignored them. He'd sent her several the night before, but she hadn't replied to them and she didn't intend to.

I don't intend to listen to his bullshit.

By the time her computer flashed that she only had ten minutes more battery, Sherri had written over ten thousand words and four very juicy chapters. She'd resurrected one of the characters she'd killed the night before, but killed him again in another even more gruesome manner, involving a corn picker.

I really shouldn't write when I'm pissed.

❧ II ❦

O n Monday morning, the crew arrived without
their supervisor.

Is the son-of-a-bitch too ashamed to face me now?

"Where's Dylan?" Sherri asked casually when she
came out onto the porch with her laptop and a cup
of coffee.

"He got a call from his daughter and had to
make an emergency trip down to Mississippi," Jeremy said. "He'll be back later this week." The
young man grinned and added, "He put me in
charge until then. Pat and Mike are gonna start on
the roof and me and the others are gonna start
pullin' down the Celotex."

That's gonna be a mess.

"Do I need to do anything inside before you start
on that?" Sherri asked, concerned because she knew
her grandparents had filled the attic of the old house
with blown-in insulation sometime in the eighties.

"No," Jeremy said with a broad grin, "we
brought tarps to cover everything." He disappeared
inside and Sherri followed him in to put away her
toaster, clean dishes from the drainer, and scoot her
coffee pot beneath the overhanging cabinet.

The brown shingle siding had been removed from the body of the house, revealing silver-gray hewn logs with a cement-like substance between them. Aside from the modern storm windows, doors, and roofing, the house now looked like a log cabin. Today, some of the men were unloading extension ladders to climb to the roof and begin stripping away the old shingles.

Insulated green metal panels had been delivered the week before and would be installed as soon as the old shingles were removed, and the decking inspected for soft spots and leaks. The new window and doors were expected to arrive any day along with green shutters to match the roof.

Sherri returned to the porch swing wrapped in a warm sweater against the morning chill and checked her email. She frowned when she saw one from Dylan, but she opened it.

I'm so sorry about what I said the other night, Sherri. I don't blame you for being mad. Believe it or not, I meant it as a compliment, though. That was the best time I've had in a damned long time. It was spontaneous and hot. You made me feel like a horny kid again. I hope you can forgive my diarrhea of the mouth

I must make a trip down south. My grandson fell off his bike and broke his arm. He needs surgery and my daughter wanted me down there with them. Please tell me you forgive me.

Dylan

Sherri rolled her eyes and sighed, unsure she was in a forgiving mood yet. She checked the rest of her mail, deleting the majority without opening it. Rather than going to her Facebook page, Sherri jumped directly into her manuscript.

After reading and editing what she'd written over the weekend, Sherri felt satisfied with her progress on the new project. Writing in the paranormal genre was something new, but she was enjoying it.

Unlike the historical fiction she had been writing, she had to do very little research and she could allow her imagination to run wild. Her recent experiences with the supernatural gave her a baseline and the rest, she pulled from old movies she'd seen or books she'd read.

As she sent chapters to Inga, she got nothing but rave reviews about how chilling they were.

Keep this up and we're gonna have Hollywood contracts in our future!

Sherri doubted that, but it was nice to hear. What she really wanted was to be able to tag her name with 'Bestselling Author". Didn't every writer?

As the day progressed, Sherri decided to make a trip into Barrett. She needed a few groceries and the construction noise was beginning to get on her nerves.

I'm going into town," she told Jeremy as he began to climb the ladder to inspect the work on the roof.

"Oh," he said and stopped halfway up the ladder, "Dylan told me to tell you to check out the back of the store at New Again, if you went into town."

"Why?" She asked. New Again was an antique store that had opened in the old Western Auto building in Barrett.

Jeremy shrugged his shoulders. "No idea."

What now?

Sherri drove into town, found what she needed at the IGA and then drove to the brick building once housing the Western Auto. Her grandfather had purchased all his hardware there and it brought back fond memories. A painted wooden sign with 'New Again Antiques' stenciled on it had replaced the red glass one from her childhood memories.

Paw-Paw loved this store when it was the Western Auto.

Inside, antiques and collectables littered the cramped aisles. Sherri couldn't see the black and white tiles she remembered on the floor for the dingy scuffs. She thought the man who had run the hardware store would be shocked at the sight. The store Sherri remembered had always been neat and tidy with brightly polished floors and wide, airy aisles.

It doesn't smell the same, either. This place always smelled a little like gasoline and grease because of the mechanic working in the back. Now it smells like musty furniture and popcorn.

"May I help you?" asked an overweight young man with a bored smile. He slouched in an old rolling office chair behind a glass display counter filled with a colorful assortment of antique fishing lures and bobbers.

"I'm just going to look around, if that's all right," Sherri said and returned his smile.

"Be my guest," he said without much enthusiasm. "If you need anything just give me a holler and I'll come runnin'."

Yah, I just bet you will.

Sherri rolled her eyes as she passed the counter and suspected the unshaven, young man hadn't run for anything in a very long while.

She strolled through the untidy store until she came to the back where antique furniture was set haphazardly about.

This place could use somebody with some merchandising experience. They have some cool stuff, but you can't really see it.

As she made her way around an oak dining room table displayed with mismatched chairs, Sherri's mouth dropped open. Beside the door leading out to the old service bays, stood the item she was certain Dylan wanted her to see. It was a wood cook stove with a robin's-egg blue enameled finish. As she got closer, Sherri saw it had been converted to use gas.

A white tag dangled from the oven handle and she turned it hesitantly for the price. Sherri gave a long sigh when she saw thirteen hundred scrawled in black ink across the tag.

This is absolutely perfect. This greenish blue will look great with the butter yellow I was planning to use on the walls in the kitchen that aren't log.

"Find something you like?" asked the young man, startling Sherri, who was engrossed, inspecting the stove. "It's been certified as safe to use by our appliance guy. You just have to have the proper gas orifice."

Sherri picked up the tag and raised an eyebrow. "How firm are you on this price?"

"Depends on what else you're gonna buy," he said with a sly grin and a wink.

"I got ya," she said. "I'll look around a little more."

When Sherri swiped her card for thirteen hundred dollars including the sales tax she had purchased the stove, a copper tone lighting fixture with white hurricane globes to hang over her kitchen table, two tall hurricane lamps converted to use electric, a cast iron fireplace set that included a painted screen, and an oil painting of a cabin with two chimneys.

Sherri thought it could have been her cabin in its early days. A covered porch ran across the front of the cabin and a yellow tabby cat was curled up on a primitive rocker.

This will look great on the wall above the couch.

"I'm going to need the stove delivered," Sherri said as she slid her bank card back into her wallet.

"Delivery will be fifty dollars extra," the young man said.

"Really?" Sherri asked snidely. "I'm carrying out all this other stuff today."

"Oh, all right," he sighed and scrawled 'Delivery included' across her computer-generated receipt. "But I can't guarantee it before the weekend."

"That's all right," she told him, "my place is a mess right now anyhow with construction. Next week any time will be cool," Sherri said as she gathered up her purchases to stow carefully in her PT.

As she drove out of town, her phone rang. It was Dylan, and she thought for a minute about punching ignore, or simply letting it ring, but she answered. "Hello."

I don't even know why I'm answering this.

"Hi, Sherri," Dylan said hesitantly. "Am I forgiven for being such a dumb ass?"

"I suppose I have to after you found the perfect stove for my kitchen."

"I thought you'd like it. How much did Kenny get you for?" he asked with a chuckle.

"Quite a bit less than the tag considering everything else I got with it."

"That's good," he sighed. "I just talked to Jeremy and they're about to wrap up for the day. They shoveled and bagged up all the ground paper insulation along with the dead mice and their droppings."

Great, I'm going to walk into a disgusting mess when I get home.

"Oh yuck," Sherri said and wrinkled her nose. "Granny always hated the mice out there and had D-Con stuck everywhere."

"Mice arc a problem with houses out in the

country," he said. "Hanta Virus isn't common around here, but if I were you, I'd mop and wipe everything down with a good disinfectant just to be safe."

"Oh, great," Sherri groaned, "I'll have to turn around and go back to the IGA."

"Go to Ace," Dylan said. "They carry some industrial-strength stuff that's better than anything you'll find in a grocery store."

Sherri pulled into a parking lot so she could turn around. "Will do," she said. "How's your grandson?"

"Went through the surgery with flying colors. They had to put a pin in his wrist."

"And your daughter?" Sherri added. "How's she doing?"

"Typical hovering mother hen," he sighed. "Carla Jean hasn't left his side and is threatening to take Kyle's bike to the dump for trying to jump ditches with it."

"Oh, my," Sherri said with a smile on her lips. "He won't be happy about that."

Talking to him was a bad idea. I miss talking to him.

"No, he won't" Dylan replied with a deep chuckle, "I'm afraid my grandson is too much like me. He enjoys living on the wild side a little too much for his mother's liking. He's definitely a boy's boy."

Sherri recognized the pride in Dylan's voice along with some longing. "You miss getting to spend time with him."

"I do," he sighed. "I wish he wasn't six hours away and regret that I don't have a place of my own so I could bring him up here during his school breaks. I wish I could take him fishing and hunting. He'd like that."

"I bet he would," Sherri said as she turned into

the Ace Hardware's parking lot. "Well, I'm at Ace. I'll talk to you later, Dylan."

"Sherri?"

"Yes?"

"I really am sorry about what I said the other night," he said apologetically. "And I enjoyed it more than you can imagine."

"I enjoyed it too, Dylan," she admitted uneasily to him and to herself.

Damnit!

"Will you let me take you out to dinner this weekend to make up for my big mouth?" He asked hesitantly. "And for the mess the guys left you with today?"

Sherri smiled. "I suppose you're forgiven," she said.

"Thanks, Sherri. I'll see you in a few days."

Sherri made her purchase of a strong disinfectant and while browsing in the hardware store, an idea struck her. She rented a floor sander and bought the strong chemicals needed to strip her floors along with two gallons of polyurethane sealant and the rollers to apply it.

I can do this. I'm tired of sitting around while everyone else works.

Beneath the old carpet they'd found wood, tongue and groove plank floors covered in several layers of enamel paint. Sherri vaguely remembered the wood floors before the carpet had been laid in the seventies and hoped they would be beautiful once the paint had been stripped away to reveal the bare wood.

Dylan talked about putting down tiles that looked like wood, but wouldn't the real thing be better? I think it would and I think I can do it. It will make me feel like I'm contributing a little to this project and not just standing by while others do all the work.

She had helped her grandfather strip, sand, and repaint the porch every Spring, and Sherri was certain she could manage the floors in the house in the evenings while the men were gone and while they were working on projects outside.

The man at Ace had loaded the heavy, awkward machine into the back of Sherri's car while she made room for her other purchases. In a clearance aisle, Sherri had found a cushion for outdoor furniture she wanted for her swing with a red gingham cover and she stuffed that in the car too.

My backside is certainly going to appreciate that.

She made her way home in a good mood with the radio blasting out Classic Rock tunes. Her mood got even better when she turned into her drive to find the new bathroom fixtures being off-loaded from a truck and stacked on the porch to await installation.

Goodbye ugly old pink bathtub! I can't wait to see you gone.

Jeremy and one of the other men had carefully removed the pink and black ceramic tiles from the bathroom floor and walls with hammers and chisels the week before. Sherri now looked forward to the removal of the matching fixtures.

Goodbye I love Lucy and hello Downton Abbey, well, Victoria, anyway.

The white clawfoot tub, pedestal sink, and the toilet with its oak flush tank were eagerly awaited. She planned to wainscot the walls with bead board and tile the floor with ceramic tiles that looked like wood planking because they had found plywood beneath the tiles.

The bathroom would end up more Victorian than Pioneer era, but Sherri didn't think she wanted to resort to an outhouse or a wooden bucket for the sake of staying true to the period. She couldn't see herself bathing in a cut-off barrel, either, or going without a shower.

I can't wait for my new bathroom to be installed. It's going to be beautiful.

Her groceries were put away in the cabinets and refrigerator by the time the bathroom fixtures were unloaded and stacked neatly on the porch to await installation. She smiled sweetly and the driver unloaded the ungainly sander from Sherri's car and carried it into the house.

By nine thirty she'd swept the floors, mopped them with the strong disinfectant, wiped down all the surfaces in the house, and vacuumed her furniture.

Though it had been covered with a canvas tarp, Sherri washed her bedding and used the vacuum on her mattress. She didn't want to take any chances with Hanta or any other viruses carried by the dehydrated rodents and the droppings left in the attic space.

It smells like a damned hospital in here now, but it's better than the dead mouse smell when I walked in.

Sherri crawled into bed that night exhausted. She didn't turn on the television and fell asleep almost as soon as her head hit the pillow.

Loud voices in the living room woke her and Sherri bolted upright in the bed. Her heart pounded for a moment, but she was getting used to these nighttime interruptions and took a few deep breaths before she pushed aside the blankets. She slid out of bed and crept to the dimly lit doorway.

What the hell is going on in there now? This is beginning to get old.

Sherri stopped and stared into the living room. It was the altered living room and Molly was there with a man. She wore the beaded blue dress Sherri had seen her in before. The man wore dark flannel trousers and a white wife-beater undershirt. His bulging muscles gleamed in the dim light from a hurricane lamp on one of the tables.

"Is he a good fuck, Molly?" A tall, muscular man with dark hair yelled as he shoved the petite blonde against the wall.

What an ass.

Sherri was surprised she could hear the girl's thoughts in her head. That had never happened before. Or had it? Sherri was confused. The whole situation confused her. Sherri put a hand to her head and rubbed her throbbing temples.

I've got to find a doctor. I bet I have a damned brain tumor or something.

"He's my goddamned cousin Louie, Miles," she yelled back and twisted out of his grasp. "But he'd probably be a damned sight better fuck than you are these days," she hissed and glowered up at him. "He doesn't spend all night guzzling gin and could probably keep it hard in me until I got mine. He doesn't just think of himself all the time like you."

I don't care if it does piss him off. He's being a jealous ass dragging me out of the Speak just because I said hello to my damned cousin.

"Don't be a loose-lipped cunt, Molly," he yelled and slapped her hard.

Sherri felt the slap as though it had been delivered to her own cheek and her hand flew up to her face. Disoriented, Sherri stared across the room. The walls were covered with the blue and pink paper like it had been the night she'd had the vision of Molly and the two women at the piano.

Is this another vision or am I dreaming this? I think I need to talk to a doctor.

Sherri heard Molly's voice in her head again.

Just stay quiet and watch, Doll. You need to see this. All of this. It's important.

"If your poor little dick would stay hard for more than a minute," Molly snarled up at the glowering man, "maybe my cunt wouldn't feel so loose, Miles."

"You shouldn't have said that, Molly," the big man yelled, glaring down at the little blonde with his fists balled in rage at his side.

Sherri rubbed her throbbing temples.

I recognize that voice. I've heard it before.

Sherri gasped when Miles pulled a switchblade from his pocket, popped out the gleaming blade, and whipped it across Molly's exposed, creamy-white throat.

The girl didn't know what he'd done until she felt him wipe the blade on her blue dress before he closed it and dropped it back into the pocket of his loose flannel trousers.

What the hell, Miles? Why did you do that? Now blood is going to get all over my new dress. I'll never be able to get that out.

Sherri watched in horror as the girl put her hand to her throat and saw her eyes go wide at the sight of the bright, red blood running through her fingers. Molly's mouth opened and Sherri watched her lips forming words that wouldn't come. She knew the girl's vocal chords had been cut with the sharp blade and she could no longer speak.

What did you do, Miles? Why did you do that?

Molly threw her arm up in frustration and blood splattered in an arc onto the wallpaper above her quivering blonde head. Miles stormed out of the room and they heard the backdoor slam. He came back in, carrying an iron prybar in one of his big hands and a hammer in the other.

For a minute, Molly thought he meant to beat her with it, but he disappeared into the dark bedroom and a sense of relief overcame her.

What are you up to in there now, Miles?

The sound of furniture being moved came from the bedroom.

Why are you moving the damned furniture, Miles? I just rearranged it and cleaned in there. You'd better put it all back the way I had it.

Sherri's head began to spin, but she knew it was the girl's head spinning from her loss of blood. She couldn't take her eyes off Molly, who'd slid down the wall to sit on the floor. Blood ran down between her breasts, soaked into the blue fabric of the short, blue dress, and pooled on the floor around her.

So, this is what happened to you, Molly. Miles Tucker cut your throat and you bled to death on the floor by the piano.

She heard wood being tossed onto the floor in the bedroom and then the heavy metal prybar dropped before Miles Tucker stomped back into the room and scooped Molly gently up into his muscular arms.

"I wish you hadn't made me do that, Molly-Doll," he said softly into her golden curls. "Now you can join the other smart-mouth cunts."

I'm so sleepy, Miles, and cold. Are you taking me to bed now? I think I drank too much tonight.

Molly drifted into unconsciousness and Sherri tried to peek into the dark bedroom but couldn't see anything. Molly was roused as Miles laid her on the damp ground in the narrow space between the floor joists.

Why are you putting me down here? I think a possum or coon must have crawled up in here and died, Miles. It stinks down here like death.

Sherri felt the cold, damp earth beneath her shoulders and on her bare legs, but a chill ran through her. She knew it was Molly feeling it and not her.

You're going to ruin my new dress in this dirty crawlspace, Miles. If I can't get my dress clean, you're gonna buy me another one, goddamnit!

Sherri gasped as she stared up from beneath the floor through Molly's drowsy eyes into Mile Tucker's face. Sherri knew that face. She'd seen that same darkly handsome face before … Dylan Roberts' face.

Oh, my god, the son-of-a-bitch killed her and closed her body up under the bedroom floor.

Sherri's head cleared and she slapped her hand over her mouth as she ran to the bathroom with the contents of her stomach, rushing up into her throat. She fell to her knees, bent over the toilet, and emptied her stomach. She knelt there and wept violently for the poor dead girl beneath the floor of her bedroom.

❉ 13 ❧

Sherri woke to pounding on her front door. She rolled over with a pain in her abdomen from throwing up and cracked one sleepy eyelid to see the red numbers on her bedside clock glowing six-thirty-five.

Oh, shit. I guess I'm going to have to get up … again. I don't even have the coffee made yet.

"I'm coming," Sherri called as she rolled off the bed and grabbed her robe. She padded across the clean, wood floors to unlock the front door and let the wide-eyed work crew inside.

"Late night, Sherri?" Jeremy asked with an impish grin.

"Yah," she said as she trudged into the kitchen. "As you can see the place has been swept, mopped, and thoroughly disinfected, so you don't have to worry about catching the Hanta Virus from our little friends in the attic."

"Great," he said in a way too chipper voice, "the tile guy will be here in a few to do the bathroom, then we can get to work installing your new stuff. I see it finally showed up. It was supposed to get here before we left yesterday but didn't."

"The guy was unloading it when I got back from town yesterday afternoon." She handed him a yellow delivery invoice. "I signed for it after he went over everything, so I knew it was all here." She smiled as Jeremy studied the invoice. "Don't you have to uninstall the old stuff first?" Sherri asked as she filled the pot with water for much-needed coffee.

"Yep, Parker is gonna get on that first thing. You should fill some pots with water, though," he said with a grin, "and use the toilet and shower now, because the water is gonna be off for a while."

Great," she groaned as she turned on the Mr. Coffee. "I'll be out in a minute or three." Sherri trudged into the bathroom and closed the door to the giggling of the workmen loitering in the kitchen while they waited for the coffee to brew.

My head is really pounding this morning. These late-night visitations are beginning to take a toll. I think I'm too old for this bullshit. I'm glad I showered last night.

She generally shared her first pot of coffee with the crew while they got their directions for the day, and Sherri got an idea of what sort of mess she could expect.

The prospect of seeing the last of the Pepto-Bismol in her bathroom should have bolstered Sherri's mood, but the early morning visit ... or vision ... or dream of Molly's murder and the sight of Miles Tucker's face and its haunting resemblance to Dylan's had unsettled Sherri.

Should I tell him about that? The subject of Miles Tucker seems to be a touchy one with Dylan.

Every time Sherri closed her eyes, she saw that face staring down as Molly had seen it in her final ghastly moments. She'd wrestled with questions most of the time since crawling back into her bed.

Was it really a vision sent by Molly or just a dream? I've been so stressed out with this project, my relationship with Dylan, and the new book. Maybe it was just a stress-induced nightmare. Maybe it has all simply been a figment of my fertile imagination. Or maybe it's a brain tumor.

Sherri flushed the toilet, returned to the kitchen, and filled her cup with strong, black coffee. She dropped into one of the chairs and took a sip, savoring the rich aroma wafting up from the cup.

"Are you feeling all right, Sherri?" Jeremy asked with concern. "Are you sick or something? You're usually up and dressed by the time we get here, and you look a little pale."

"And have the coffee made," one of the other men said with a chuckle.

"I'm sorry, guys," Sherri sighed. "It was a late night last night. Dylan said I should disinfect the place after dropping all that crap yesterday, so I stayed up late cleaning." She raised her very clean hands for them to see and then shrugged. "I think smelling the disinfectant made me a little queasy too."

"What's this for?" Jeremy asked as he rocked the handle of the floor sander. "Dylan usually has our floor guy do the stripping and sanding if that's the plan, but I thought he said something about using tile on this job."

"I thought I'd give it a go. I'd rather use the wood floors where I can for authenticity's sake," she said with a weak grin. "I helped my gramps refinish the porch every year, so I think I can handle it."

Jeremy rolled his big blue eyes and grinned at the other men in the kitchen. "A little porch like the one outside is nothing compared to a whole house, Sherri. The fumes alone in here will probably knock you out within an hour."

I have window fans for every room," she said

confidently and shrugged her shoulders. "I'll turn them to suck the fumes out while I'm working." She glanced up into the dark, open attic space and grinned. "There's a good bit more airspace in here now too."

Sherri emptied her cup and got up to refill it. She noticed the pot was close to empty and made a fresh one. "Are you guys gonna be able to get the metal on the roof before it rains again and what about the wood Dylan said they were going to line the inside with? When is that going to be installed?"

"The roof is next on the list of to do's," Jeremy said, "and the ceiling crew will be in tomorrow to get started, I think." He glanced at one of the other men who nodded. "What are you gonna need to get this project of yours started?"

"I need both stoves disconnected and moved out," Sherri said and grinned at the young man. "I cleaned out the spare bedroom last night and moved everything to the utility room, but as soon as the old fixtures are out of the bathroom I need the new ones moved in, so I can move furniture out there while I work on the floors."

"You heard the boss, boys," Jeremy said and drained his cup. "Let's get to it."

Half of them went out to begin work on the roof while others began taking out the pink bathroom fixtures and the stoves.

As Sherri filled her empty stomach with a hot, buttered bagel, Dylan called.

"Hello," she said, chewing as fast as she could so she could talk.

"So, Jeremy tells me you have a special project in the works."

A chill went down her spine at the sound of his voice. It was Miles Tucker's voice. The same stern, accusatory voice she'd heard a few hours before. She shivered and pulled her robe tighter around her body.

Get a grip, Lambert. It was probably just another dream. Get with it and come back to the here and now.

"Oh, he did, did he?" Sherri said, glaring at Jeremy as he knelt in the bathroom with a wrench in his hand, releasing the bolts connecting the toilet to the floor. She wondered when he'd had time to make the call to Dylan. Sherri suddenly felt like she had a house full of babysitters or worse—spies.

"If I'd known you wanted the floors stripped and refinished, I'd have added it to the contract and made arrangements with our floor man," Dylan said, and Sherri could imagine the grin creasing his handsome face.

"I don't think I can afford any more additions to my contract, Dylan," she sighed. "Until the funds from the sale of my condo come through, I need to do as much on the cheap as I can." Sherri paused to consider her next words. "I think I can afford a little sweat equity."

"Bobby hates that term," Dylan said and chuckled.

"I just bet he does," Sherri said as she refilled her cup, switched off the pot, and walked outside into the crisp Fall morning. She wanted some privacy away from all the ears in the house. The brisk, fresh air helped Sherri to clear her head some, as well.

"Jeremy said you don't look well and were still in bed when they got there this morning." Sherri heard the concern in his voice and was touched. "Are you feeling all right?"

How can he be so sweet and thoughtful one day and such an ass another?

"I'm fine," she sighed and glanced toward the

house. "I'm just tired. I was up late last night cleaning. Didn't he tell you that too?"

They'd probably have me committed if I told them why I was really so tired. Seeing ghosts committing murder in the living room and burying the body beneath the bedroom floor doesn't sound very sane.

"He did." Dylan paused. "When I said you needed to disinfect the place, I didn't mean you had to do it all in one night."

"I know," she said, "but I was on a roll and when I get something in my head, I have to get it done."

"Like the floors?" he asked, and Sherri could imagine his grinning face.

Miles Tucker's face.

"Yes," she sighed with a little smile on her lips, "like the floors. I want to see what they look like before I decide what I'm going to do with the walls."

"Have you decided on cabinets yet? We need to get those ordered, too."

"Again," she sighed, "it depends on what the floors look like."

"OK," he said. "I told Jeremy to give you all the help you need with your project. He has a full crew there and we're on schedule with everything. I'll see you in a couple of days."

"Thanks, Dylan, but isn't Bobby gonna be upset about that?"

"This is my project," he snapped. "I run the damned crews; not Bobby." Sherri heard him take a breath. "I gotta go now. They're releasing Kyle today, and I'm driving him and Carla Jean home. I'll talk to you later," he said.

Bye," Sherri said and disconnected.

Wow, mentioning Bobby really pushed his buttons. Good to know.

Sherri tucked the phone in the pocket of her

robe, glanced up at the men joking and laughing as they nailed roof panels in place, and returned to the house where they were struggling with getting the old pink tub through the bathroom door.

Should I have told him how much I miss him? Should I tell him about my visions and how much he looks like Miles Tucker?

❧ 14 ❧

I can't get her off my damned mind. She's the most exciting woman I've ever been with. Then I had to open my damned mouth and put my foot in it. She's probably never gonna let me between her legs again and I don't know if I can deal with that.

Dylan sat in traffic on the northbound interstate. There must have been an accident somewhere ahead. He'd driven Carla Jean and Kyle home, seen them settled in, and then said his goodbyes. He needed to get back. Sherri's project was getting out of hand and wreaking havoc with his carefully planned schedule.

He'd learned early-on, not to allow the home-owner to start side-projects of their own. Sherri's floor project could throw everything into a downhill spiral if he didn't get back and put things back on schedule. Bobby wanted to use her cabin renovation in the company's holiday advertising. That meant it needed to be finished or very close to finished by Thanksgiving.

Too bad he can't order up snow. That green roof would look great in the photos with a little snow on it.

The cars ahead of him began to move and Dylan

slipped his sunglasses back in place. As he drove, he thought about how well the cabin was coming along. He'd ordered some pine lodgepole posts to replace the old white turned posts on the porch. Once those, the new windows with their primitive shutters, and the doors were installed, the place wouldn't look anything like the house his mother had taken him to as a child.

It is already unrecognizable without that horrid shingle siding. It looks like a log cabin now.

"That's an evil house and our family's greatest shame," Marilyn Tucker Roberts had told her ten-year-old son as they sat in her new red Buick Electra on the gravel road.

"Why?" a young Dylan had asked, staring at the simple brown house. A little redheaded girl with a book in her hands stared at them from the porch swing. "It's just an old house." He turned to stare at his mother with her beehive hairdo. "Is it haunted or something?"

"Or something," she sighed. "My family lived in that house once."

"You lived in a junky, little house like that?" He asked in wide-eyed surprise. The Roberts family lived in a spacious new split-level on one of the best streets in Barrett. Dylan couldn't picture his mother living in this tacky little farmhouse with a black cinder driveway and chickens wandering loose in the yard.

"For a little while," she admitted. "but we moved into Barrett when I was about your age, but my uncle continued to live here with his trashy women."

"I guess living out here in the country with chickens in the yard is shameful," he said and suddenly felt sorry for the girl in the swing. It must be terrible to be so poor.

"My uncle was a very bad man and he lived

here," his mother mumbled. "And he was related to us, Dylan."

"Who?" Dylan asked, excited. "Was he a cattle rustler or stagecoach robber?" The only bad men Dylan could relate to were the ones on *Gun Smoke*, *Wagon Train*, and in John Wayne movies. "Was he a bank robber like Jessie James and did he get strung up?"

"He never robbed banks," his mother said. "But he was hanged for his crimes."

"Really?" Dylan asked, staring at his mother in awe. "You're related to a man who was hanged? Did he really murder someone?"

"He did," his mother sighed sadly, but then her voice turned hard. It was the voice she used when she was mad at him or Bobby. "And he's related to you and Bobby too. That's why you need to know about him. His name was Miles Tucker. He was hanged for murder and I never want to hear you talk about him ... ever." She grabbed his shoulder and yanked Dylan around in the seat to face her. "Do you understand me, Dylan? That man was my uncle and a disgrace to our family. I never want to hear you admit that you are related to him ... never."

Her fingers dug into Dylan's shoulder and brought tears to his young eyes. "Yes, ma'am," he said solemnly.

"Good," she said and released his shoulder.

Dylan turned to stare at the girl in the swing as he brushed away tears. His mother put the car into gear and threw gravel as she spun the tires of the big, red Buick and drove toward the blacktop that would take them back into Barrett.

Oh, my god, that little girl must have been Sherri. She was so tiny back then in that swing, reading her book. Now she sits in it and writes them.

Dylan had never mentioned Miles Tucker to anyone but had looked him up at the library while in high school. He remembered feeling embarrassed when Tucker's name had been brought up during a history class. He'd been tempted to raise his hand and admit the man was his relative, but the memory of his mother's stern face in the car that day had stopped him. Tucker had even been on the test.

Who was the last man executed by hanging in the state?

Dylan would never forget the answer to that question.

He found a book about the man and had been surprised to read that he'd been a notorious bootlegger and the leader of a gang of outlaws that distributed the illegal liquor during Prohibition. Tucker had eventually been arrested, tried, and hanged in 1930 for ordering the murders of rivals and some law enforcement officers. The officers, however, were thought to have been on the payroll of the rival gang.

Now I'm renovating his damned house.

Dylan didn't think their mother had ever told Bobby about Tucker and had never taken him to the house. Dylan didn't know why, and he'd never mentioned it to him either. He hadn't told his mother about where he was working now and struggled with it.

Should I tell her I'm working on her childhood home and ask her if Bobby knows about our relationship to Tucker? Would he want that getting out in his big holiday spread? Dylan could see the headlines now: Realistic Renovations revamps house of notorious murderer and great-uncle.

His mother would certainly love that. He decided he would have to discuss it with her and Bobby soon. They say no publicity is bad publicity, but Dylan had to wonder if Bobby would feel that way.

As he neared the exit into Barrett, Dylan's mind returned to the little, redheaded girl in the porch swing and the woman she'd become. In his thoughts, he pulled the woman onto his hard cock again and relived the amazing sex they'd had in his car.

How many nights this week had he jacked off to visions of her standing in front of him in those thigh-high hose with no underwear on and her big tits?

Why can't I get her off my mind? She's like a walking, fucking wet dream. I swear this car still smells like her pussy and I get hard thinking about her. She was so damned hot!

❀ 15 ❀

Sherri strolled through the brightly lit house, admiring the glossy floors. With the help of Jeremy and his five men under the direction of the floor guy, Paul, the project had gone amazingly fast. In a matter of hours, room-by-room, the floors had been stripped, sanded, and coated with layers of clear polyurethane.

The men had worked together to reveal beautiful floors that were a combination of pine and ash woods. The polyurethane, when it had been applied, brought the wood to life, accentuating the grain, and bringing out colors Sherri hadn't noticed before. When it dried, the coating gleamed in the Autumn sunlight, streaming through the windows.

This is exactly what I hoped for. Dylan is going to be so pleased.

Sherri couldn't have been more pleased. She couldn't imagine why anybody would have wanted to cover them with paint in the first place. As she moved through the living room, skating in her socked feet, something caught Sherri's eye and she stopped to study it.

Her breath caught in her throat as she stared at a

discolored spot marring the wood planks. In the exact spot where she'd seen Molly slide to the floor, Sherri saw the clear outline of ass cheeks. It reminded her of a Xeroxed image of a bare ass someone had once made at an office Christmas party. Sherri knew; however, this image had been made with blood and she knew whose blood.

Maybe this is the reason why the floors were painted. Maybe Miles painted them when he couldn't clean up the blood.

Her good mood faded. Sherri switched off the lights and made her way into the bedroom. She undressed and walked to the bed. As she neared it, Sherri stared at another spot on the boards. In a section, roughly five feet by six feet, the planks had cracks and splits. The men had taken extra care to sand them smooth so Sherri wouldn't snag her feet on splinters.

Paul had told her it looked as if the flooring had been pried up at some point and then replaced with the same boards. Perhaps there had been a problem in the crawl space beneath the floor.

Sherri knew there had been no problem and swallowed hard as she hopped over the boards to get into her bed.

"Are you down there, Molly?" Sherri said into the darkness as she shivered and pulled the blankets up about her shoulders. "If you are, I promise to find you and give you the proper burial you deserve."

"Please, don't forget Tillie and Maudie, Doll," Molly's disembodied voice said. Sherri gave a start and pulled the blankets tighter beneath her trembling chin. "They have people waitin' too. Promise you'll have a preacher say words over them too."

"I will," Sherri whispered. "I promise you I will."

"Make that man of yours take a good look at

what's left of me, Doll. Make him look at what *he* did to us."

Why on Earth would she want that?

"Why?" Sherri asked in confusion. "Dylan isn't Miles Tucker."

Molly made no reply in the dark room. Sherri had a hard time falling asleep. She wracked her brain, attempting to put some meaning to Molly's words.

I know Dylan has an uncanny resemblance to Miles Tucker, but he's nothing like that drunken murderer. I think he's a good man.

Sherri set her alarm for five so there wouldn't be a repeat of the morning before. The vision of Molly's murder replayed over and over behind Sherri's eyes until she finally dozed off, but she tossed and turned with restless dreams of Molly for most of the night.

When her alarm sounded, Sherri came full awake and rolled out of bed. She rummaged through her dresser drawers and pulled out a clean pair of jeans and a sweater. Her footsteps echoed in the empty house as Sherri padded across the gleaming new floors to the bathroom.

She shivered for a moment as she gazed around the newly installed bathroom. A black oval ring had been suspended from the ceiling over the clawfoot tub for a shower curtain. A large black shower head now protruded from the wall and she wacked her head on the oak flush tank over the new toilet seat.

It looks great, but maybe I should have given that a bit more consideration.

Sherri rubbed at the tender spot on her head as she sat on the toilet and admired the new bathroom. The ceramic tiles Paul had installed matched the actual wood floors in the kitchen perfectly. When the bead board wainscot was installed and the walls were painted, Sherri knew the little room would be everything she'd hoped for. The new windows hadn't arrived yet so the walls would have to wait until then.

Sherri splashed some water on her face and ran a brush through her disheveled curls before making her way into the kitchen to start a pot of coffee. The crew would be there soon, and she wanted to be dressed and ready for the day when they arrived.

Her head throbbed and she wondered if it was from lack of a restful night's sleep or all the chemicals she'd inhaled the day before. She poured a cup of coffee and smiled as she smelled the rich aroma. Coffee always helped with her headaches.

The day before had been so busy, Sherri hadn't touched her laptop. She cringed at the thought of going through the accumulated emails as she walked into the living room to get the computer and carry it back into the kitchen. When she went into her email account, Sherri rolled her eyes when she saw over ninety-eight. She knew the majority would be deleted without opening, but there were a few things she had been waiting for.

One of those was a notification from her realtor in Palm Springs, telling Sherri the closing on her condo had taken place and the funds deposited into her account. She smiled when she ran down the list and saw an email from the realtor and another from her bank. The closing had gone without a hitch and her bank account had a fresh injection of funds. Sherri was glad to be finished with the final thing tying her to the desert southwest.

Now I can breathe a little easier and not worry that I can't finish this house if something unexpected pops up.

With the certainty of funds in her bank, Sherri sat staring at the kitchen. Now that the floors were finished, she'd have to deal with the cabinets. She leafed through a catalogue and studied the pages she'd marked. A display of primitive, pine cabinets held her interest, though she also liked a set with mullioned glass doors.

Do I really want people to see all the mess in my cabinets? What people? I never have company.

In frustration, Sherri set aside the catalogue and stared at the bare wall where the gas range had been. She glanced into the living room and studied the fireplace, revealed when they'd stripped away the paneling. Golden stratified sandstone slabs had been stacked to make the fireplace.

Now that the old gas space heater had been removed Sherri could get a good look at it for the first time. The men had pried away the boards sealing the blackened fire box and they'd been happy to find it hadn't been mortared in. The carcasses of several dead birds and the remains of some nests had to be cleaned out of it. At some point the mantle had been removed, but Sherri knew exactly what it should look like. She would set Jeremy on a mission to find a replacement.

Jeremy had assured Sherri that once the hole in the flue had been filled in, she should be able to safely have a fire. He'd searched the area around the property and collected some stones, carefully matching them to the ones in the fireplace. It had taken some doing, but the young man had done a beautiful job of patching the hole.

I've always wanted a real wood-burning fireplace, but in California with all the Eco-Nazis the restrictions had only allowed for gas.

Sherri thought back to the night of her vision of Molly and the women at the piano. The fireplace still needed a mantle and a raised hearth stone. She made a mental note to speak to Paul about building a hearth stone to match the fireplace and then turned her attention back to the wall in the kitchen. Layers of dingy wallpaper splattered with decades of grease covered the wall. It was bubbled and cracked in several places.

This mess has got to go.

Sherri knew what she needed to do, and she returned to the bathroom where she dressed in the jeans and a sweater. As she went through her purse to find her wallet, the crew arrived.

"Wipe your feet on that rug," Sherri yelled as the men opened the screen door. "I don't want you tracking mud in on my new floors."

"Yes, ma'am," Jeremy called back, but Sherri could hear the mirth in his voice. "Nice to see you're up and at 'em this morning," he said when he saw Sherri sitting at the table fully dressed. "You get some rest last night?"

"Yes, I did," she said as the men began to fill their coffee cups. "What are you guys working on today?"

"They delivered the doors and windows to the office yesterday," Jeremy said, "so we're gonna start on those today and the crew will be here today to start putting up the insulated panels before the tongue and groove goes up on the ceiling."

"That's wonderful," Sherri said excitedly. "I need to run into town this morning, so you're in charge, Jeremy."

"Do you want us to bring the stoves back in?" One of the men asked.

Her eyes darted to the bare wall. "No, not yet. I want to peel off that old wallpaper first." She noticed her breath as she spoke. "If you're cold, you can build a fire in the fireplace, I guess. We're not putting the old heater back into the living room."

Why would I when I have a beautiful fireplace?

"You're gonna freeze to death in here, Sherri," Jeremy fretted. "What are you gonna do for heat?"

Sherri smiled at his concern. "I'm having a heat pump installed. They promised me they'd be out here to do it before Thanksgiving."

"That's next Thursday," someone said. "Are we doing the duct work, or are they?"

"They are," Jeremy said firmly. "We don't do that climbing in the damned rafter shit." He turned to one of the younger crew members. "Benny, get a fire goin' in that fireplace. It's colder than a witch's tit in here. There is plenty of cutoff stuff in that pile out back."

They had burned one pile of trash in the spot by the rusted barrels a few weeks earlier, but another had accumulated as the work on the cabin renovation continued.

"Sure thing," the young man said and went out the back door.

Sherri admired Jeremy's leadership abilities. She could see why Dylan had left the tall, skinny blond in charge rather than one of the older men. She shut down her laptop and closed it.

I need to get this trip to town taken care of and then get back and get some work done. Inga says I've been slacking. She wants three full chapters to send to the publisher before the weekend.

"I'm gonna take off after I finish this cup of coffee," she said. "I'll only be gone for a couple of hours."

"All right," Jeremy said with a grin, "take your time. We'll be here all day and Dylan might show. I think he got back in town last night."

Sherri was surprised to hear that, and her heart picked up a pace at the prospect of seeing Dylan again. She thought back to the kiss at the Best Western and then to the sex in his car in the driveway. Her nipples began to throb, and she rushed outside to her car.

You're too old for this high school crush nonsense, Lambert. Get over it. It will probably never happen again. Dylan Roberts was just another one-night stand. Just one of too many.

She started her car, turned up the radio, and backed out of the drive. Unfortunately, she couldn't get Dylan off her mind as she drove to the Home Depot. She wondered how he'd like the floors and what he'd think of the new bathroom. Suddenly what Dylan would think was more important to Sherri than most anything else.

As she pulled into the Home Depot parking lot, Sherri heard Molly's voice in her head reminding her about Dylan's bad blood and a shiver ran down her spine.

Get hold of yourself and get back on track. You've got more important things to attend to than your stupid sex life. You have a career now to think about.

Sherri took a deep breath, grabbed her purse, and walked into the store. It was early, but the store was busy. She inhaled the refreshing scent of freshly cut lumber, took a cart, and pushed it to the aisle she wanted.

Sherri had an idea of what she wanted and after a few minutes of study, she found exactly what she needed to accomplish the look she hoped for in her new kitchen. She hefted heavy boxes onto her cart and pushed it through a few other aisles, picking up this and that. She had always loved shopping at The Home Depot.

"Sherri Lambert?" A male voice called from behind her as she stood in the checkout line. "Is that really you?"

Sherri turned to see a heavy-set, balding man standing behind a cart filled with plumbing supplies. "Yes?" she said, not recognizing the man.

"It's Tom," he said as he pushed the cart closer to her. "Tom Garret. I heard you'd moved back to the area."

Sherri gaped at the man. Could this really be the Tommy Garrett she'd had such a crush on all those years ago? Her Tommy had had a full head of thick wavy hair and a trim waistline. He'd looked so hot in his tight, white softball uniform pants. This man looked like he needed to wear the equipment bags.

Well, it has been over forty years and that would make him almost sixty-five now.

"Oh," she said, forcing a smile, "hi, Tom. I didn't recognize you. It's been a while."

Either Laura is a good cook, or you spend a lot of time munching onion rings at Sonic.

"Yah," he sighed, "it's definitely been a while. I was sorry to hear about your grandpa. He was a good old bird and so was your grandma."

Not good enough for you to turn up at their funeral or send flowers, though.

Sherri may have missed this Tommy Garrett at the funeral, but she hadn't seen his name on the guest book from the funeral home or on any of the cards from the arrangements that had been sent.

"That he was," Sherri said, "and he always thought highly of you."

Though you turned out to be a pig.

"So," he said and bent in closer to Sherri, "I hear you're a writer now. I read that article about you in the paper and looked up your books on Amazon."

He reached out to touch her hair. "Pretty racy stuff. You write that from experience or make it all up?"

I hear that question from every man I talk to. I'd love to hear something original some time.

"The number one rule of writing is 'write what you know'," she said as she handed the cashier her debit card.

"Why don't you and me get together sometime," he said with a lascivious grin, "and you can show me what tricks you've learned since the last time we were together in a bed?"

Yah, right. Not in a million fucking years.

"Are you and Laura still married?" Sherri asked loudly as she pushed her cart toward the door. She didn't wait for his answer.

What a creep. Some things and some people never change. He's still an ass. I can't believe I ever crushed on him like I did and let him take my virginity. Give yourself credit, Lambert. You were only fourteen and thought you were in love.

As she drove home, Sherri wondered who Tommy had been talking to and then she remembered Candi mentioning him at The Best Western. That couldn't be good. Candi would have put a salacious spin on her writing, though the article in the Barrett paper had said she wrote Erotic Romances along with Historical Fiction.

If Tommy had gone to Amazon and opened one of the free sample reads there, he could have found a few where the erotic action started in the first few chapters. Sherri rolled her eyes and rubbed her temple.

Maybe I should rethink that. Maybe I should always start slow and let it build.

When she walked into the house, the place was in a state of chaos. Wood screeched as windows were being removed and hammers pounded in the attic space as the insulated panels were being installed.

"What ya think, Sherri?" Jeremy asked as he carried freshly cut boards across the room to where one of the men was installing a window beside the fireplace.

"It's amazing," she said with a broad smile. "You guys really get on it."

"It's what the boss pays us for," he said. "Hey," he said and began pulling Sherri toward the piano, "look what we found when we started pulling back the old wallpaper around the window on this wall."

Sherri stopped and a chill ran up her spine when she recognized the layer of faded pink and blue paper. "What?" she asked nervously. "It's just more old wallpaper."

"This," Jeremy said, pointing to an arch of dark brown splotches on the paper. "It looks like blood spatter to me."

Oh, my.

"You watch too many damned crime shows on television, Jeremy," one of the men said with a chuckle. "We've been hearing all week how he thinks that dark spot on the floor there," he said and pointed to a spot now covered by a canvas tarp, "was a blood pool or some such nonsense and now he sees brown spots on old wallpaper and says it's blood spatter."

He's observant and he's exactly right. It's Molly's blood. I saw it happen right before my eyes.

Sherri took a deep breath and patted Jeremy's shoulder She wished she could tell him what she knew but thought better of it. "This is an old house," she said. "No telling what kind of secrets it has."

"You see," Jeremy said, "Sherri believes me."

The screen door opened, and Dylan stepped inside. "Sherri believes what?" he asked with his brow furrowed in concern.

Sherri went into the kitchen and filled two cups with coffee while the men explained. Dylan walked in, shaking his head. "That damned boy has one hell of an imagination."

"You don't think there could be anything to it?" Sherri asked as she handed him a cup. "One of the state's most notorious criminals used to live here."

She watched as Dylan's face darkened. "You know about that?"

Sherri nodded as she took a seat at the table. "Louis told me when I went to the library to check this place out. He told me about Tucker and recommended a book."

I know you saw me reading it.

"Oh, I see," he said. "Did he tell you anything else?"

Sherri shook her head. "He just suggested that book about Tucker," she said, "and I checked it out, but it didn't offer much. Nothing about the house or its origins anyway."

About as much as you're gonna offer about Miles Tucker. Why all the secrecy? He's been dead for decades.

Dylan rubbed at his mustache and poked his head into the bathroom. "This turned out nice. What do you think?"

Sure, change the subject.

"A hell of a lot better than that Pepto-Bismol mess I had in there before. What do you think of the floors?"

Dylan glanced down and smiled. "They look great," he said, "but I hope that's the last side-job you have planned during this project. It screws with my schedule something fierce."

Sherri glanced at the wall where the old range had sat. "Only one more," she said meekly with downcast eyes.

"Oh, my lord," Dylan groaned and ran a hand through his dark, wavy hair. "What now?"

"Well," she said and grinned, "since the fireplace in here was removed at some point, I bought stone to match the fireplace in there to put on the wall here where the new stove is gonna go."

Dylan studied the wall, glanced into the living room, and then smiled. "That's a great idea. I wish I'd thought of it." He sipped his coffee. "Have you decided on cabinets yet?"

Sherri shuffled through the stack of catalogues on the table and found the one with cabinets. "These," she said, "with an Irish farm sink and the dark Victorian gooseneck faucet set." Sherri watched his face as he studied her selections. "I know it's more Victorian than Pioneer, but so is the bathroom, so I thought it would be all right."

"Good choice," he said and nodded. "I'll get them ordered today." Dylan took her hand. "You gonna let me take you to dinner tonight?"

"That sounds good," she said. "What should I wear?"

Dylan grinned. "It's just Applebee's," he said, "but if you wear that outfit you wore to the Westie, I can't guarantee your virtue will remain intact."

"Sweetie," she giggled and thought of Tommy Garrett, "I haven't been virtuous for a damned long time."

"I'm not touching that one," Dylan said as he raised his hands in a defensive posture and turned in his chair.

"Jeremy," he called into the other room, "Sherri has some stuff in the back of her car that needs to come in here for a project."

"Sure, boss," he yelled back over the hammering. "Right on it."

The tall, skinny young man poked his head into the kitchen. "Another project?" he said with an impish grin. "Bobby's not gonna be happy. He wants all the projects on a job."

Uh, oh, that might not be good.

"We're well ahead of schedule," Dylan chided. "Just go unload the damned car." He emptied his coffee cup and stood. "I better get back to the office and get these cabinets ordered." Dylan bent and kissed her cheek. "I'll be here to pick you up at seven."

"See you then," Sherri said and watched his behind in his tight jeans as he walked away. Her mind wandered back to their night together in his car and her heart fluttered in her chest.

You're too old for this schoolgirl nonsense, Lambert. Get hold of yourself and grow up.

"Where do you want this stuff, Sherri?" Jeremy asked as he brought in the boxed tiles on a hand truck.

"Along the wall there is fine," she said.

"What ya gonna be doin' in here now?"

Sherri went on to explain her plans for the wall behind the stove. "I want to have it done before they deliver it."

"It's an easy enough project," he said. "Me and Ben can help if you want. We've been workin' with Paul on some sidejobs and have picked up a thing or two."

"Thanks for the offer, Jeremy, but I think I want to tackle this one on my own I've done some tile work before on my place in California."

❧ 17 ❧

After the crew left for the day, Sherri showered and moussed her curls. She stood at her closet for a long time, trying to decide what to wear. Did she want to go for sexy or comfortable? Why couldn't there be a middle ground between the two?

In the end, she settled for a pair of tight black jeans, a frilly white bustier, and a black denim jacket. On her feet, she wore shiny black cowboy boots. Sherri examined herself in the mirror after applying her makeup and smiled.

Not too casual, but not too slutty either, though the bustier pushes the girls up there front and center. He likes that cowboy look. He should go for this.

A spritz or two of her favorite perfume finished things off and she went in to wait for Dylan on the couch. She glanced up and saw the brown arc of spots on the wall and she expelled a long sigh. Her eyes went to the dark spot on the floor where Molly's blood had pooled and soaked into the boards. Paul had said the stain added character, but Sherri wondered if he'd say the same thing if he'd known where it came from the way she did.

Dylan's knock brought her back to the present

and she jumped to her feet. Sherri glanced at her laptop and smiled.

Sorry, fellas, you'll just have to wait for my attention until tomorrow. I think I want a flesh and blood man with a nice ass tonight.

Sherri picked up her purse, flipped on the porch light, and answered the door. She watched Dylan's eyes go wide.

"Damn, woman," he sighed as he stared down at her cleavage. "That outfit might not be good for your virtue either."

"Who says I want it to be," she said as she stepped out onto the porch and pulled the door shut behind her.

"Well, all right, then," he said with a broad smile and took her hand to walk with her to the car.

"Bobby let you have the nice wheels again?"

"We're gonna be talkin' about this project, aren't we?" he asked as he opened the door.

"Absolutely," Sherri said.

"It's a business dinner then," he said as he closed the door.

Sherri buckled her seatbelt and watched him walk around the front of the luxury automobile, open the driver's side door, and drop into the seat. He wore black jeans as well, a white shirt with a black leather vest, and his black cowboy hat.

Maybe I should have asked him what he planned to wear.

"You look really hot tonight, Sherri," he said as he started the car.

"You look good too, Dylan."

"Thanks," he said and backed out of the drive. "I got those cabinets ordered. They were in stock and will be shipped this week. We should have this project wrapped in another week if everything comes in on time."

All right, we've officially discussed business.

"That's great," she said. "It will be nice to have a little peace and quiet around this place."

"I guess we've been messing with your writing schedule, haven't we?"

"My agent just pitched my next three-book series to the publisher," Sherri said.

"Oh, yah, how'd that go?" he asked and turned onto the main road into Barrett.

Sherri smiled. "They want it and offered an ungodly advance."

"That's great," he said with a grin. "What's ungodly in the book writing business?"

"Low six figures," she said with a pause before adding, "per book."

Dylan turned his head and whistled. "I'm in the wrong line of work. What's this series about?"

"A family of witches in the Louisiana bayous," she said. "If it goes over well, I could stretch it to more than three books, I'm sure."

"Wow," he said.

"Inga—my agent, is pitching it to some screenwriters in Hollywood too for a movie deal or maybe a television series."

"You're gonna be rich," he said. "You'll be out of poor little Barrett again before you know it for the bright lights of Hollywood or LA."

"I don't think so," she sighed and shook her head. "I've had my fill of big city life and you couldn't pay me to live in California again. I need the peace and quiet here to write." She smiled at the handsome man across the car. "I think I've found just what I want right here."

Oh, get a grip, Lambert. You don't get Happily-Ever-Afters. You just get quick, hot sex and usually a broken heart.

Dylan turned his head and smiled at Sherri. "I

hope you're right," he said and stretched his hand across the console.

Sherri took it and returned his smile. "I couldn't think of anything I might want more," she said and squeezed his warm hand.

The car slowed and Sherri peeked up to see the Applebee's. There weren't many cars in the lot on a weeknight and Sherri was glad of that.

I don't need a repeat of the night at the Best Western. Well, maybe the sex afterward, but not in the car like a couple of horny teenagers.

They walked into the restaurant and the hostess led them to a booth in the back where two other couples sat.

"Oh, for Christ's sake," she heard Dylan hiss and she glanced at the occupied booths.

Sherri saw Candi grinning at them from one booth and Tommy Garrett from the other.

"You can say that again," Sherri said as Tommy stared at her chest, grinning lasciviously.

"Well, look who's here to eat at our little Applebee's," Candi sneered. "The famous Whiskey Treat."

"Give it a rest, Candi," Dylan snarled as Laura Garrett turned to stare at them.

This is gonna be worse than the damned Best Western.

"You wanna go somewhere else?" Dylan asked before taking a seat.

Sherri watched Candi's grinning face. "No, I'm not gonna let trailer trash run me away from a good meal."

Dylan sat, smiled, and took her hand beneath the table. "Good for you," he whispered and kissed her cheek.

"My mother is still checking into having that trashy book of yours pulled off the shelves, Sherri."

"Oh, yah," Sherri shot back, "which one? I've published over a dozen."

Candi shot to her feet. "You know which one. The one where you trashed me, my family, and everyone at Barrett High." She turned to the other table. "I even know which characters in that book are supposed to be Laura and Tommy."

I'm sure they would too if they read it.

"Sherri got some great news today from her agent in New York," Dylan chirped as he pretended to study the menu. "She just sold that book to a producer who is going to make it into a show on the CW Network. Isn't that great?"

The color drained from Candi's plump face and she shot to her feet. "I'm gonna sue your ass off, Lambert," she hissed, "and so will half this town." Candi left her table and stormed over to stand beside Dylan. "That book defames you as much as it does me, Dylan. I can't believe you'd be seen out in public with her. She spread her legs for half the town. Your mother must be furious with you."

"It's only defamation if it's untrue and as I recall, we were pretty bad kids in high school. Didn't they call us the Snot Squad because we were so hateful to people? And my mother lets me choose my own dates, by the way."

"I'm sure she wouldn't be very happy about this little tramp," Candi snorted.

"That's exactly what she used to say about you, Candi. She said there was only one reason she could think of why I'd want to date a dirty tramp like you," Dylan shot back at Candi. Her husband grinned and gave Dylan a thumbs-up behind his wife's back.

"That's a mean thing to say, Dylan. Your mother always liked me, and I think she was upset when we broke up because she thought I was going to be her daughter-in-law someday."

Dylan snorted. "My mother couldn't stand you, Candi, and she bought me a new car when we broke up as a reward for finally coming to my senses."

Candi turned to her grinning husband. "Are you ready to go? I've lost my appetite."

"I haven't," her husband snapped and didn't move from his seat. "Wait for me in the car while I eat if you don't want to sit with me in here."

She grabbed her purse from the seat and stormed out. "Truth hurts, don't it, Candi?" Her husband called after her. He turned back to Dylan. "We're gonna have to coordinate our dinner plans more often, my friend," he said with a smile and a wink. "Life goes much easier at home after someone's put my dear wife in her place and you folks do a good job of pickin' her up and droppin' her right down where she belongs."

Their dinner arrived and they enjoyed it in peace. The Garretts left without speaking, though Tommy nodded at Dylan and Sherri could feel his eyes riveted to her cleavage. Candi's husband walked out after finishing both his and Candi's plates.

"That was fun," Dylan said as they walked back to the car.

Maybe for you.

"It was exhausting," Sherri sighed and slid into the seat. "I don't enjoy confrontations."

They rode back to the house with the radio on the classic rock station, listening to Led Zeppelin. Stairway to Heaven set the mood for the ride.

"I love that song," Sherri said as the final soft guitar licks ended and a commercial for a local tire service jolted the airwaves.

"It's okay," Dylan said, "but I'm more of a Sky-nard fan."

"I like the southern rock too," she said, "but Stevie Ray does it for me."

"The Allmans are good too," Dylan said as he bobbed his head to Desperado.

Sherri sat, staring at Dylan's silhouette as they drove down the country roads with the harvest moon shining bright in the Autumn sky. The trees had lost their leaves and the bare branches reached out with skeletal fingers from the hedgerows. Witchy Woman began to play, and a chill ran down her spine.

"Why didn't you tell me about Miles Tucker and my house?" She asked the question that had nagged at her since the night at the Best Western.

Dylan's head stopped moving to the music and he turned to stare at Sherri. His dark glare brought about another chill. She'd seen those dark eyes before —Miles Tucker's eyes.

"You know we were related?"

Sherri nodded. "Louis mentioned it and when I went back to that book and studied the photographs, I noticed a strong resemblance between the two of you."

I'm not gonna tell you how I really saw the resemblance.

Dylan put a hand to his face and rubbed his mustache. "Really?"

"You look just like him," she said.

"Wow," he sighed and turned the volume on the radio down. "He was my mom's uncle. She brought me out to your house once when I was a kid. We sat in the car out front and she told me about him." Dylan turned into her drive and parked in front of the porch. "She told me never to talk about him because he was a disgrace to the family." Dylan exhaled a long breath. "I guess she put the fear of God into me, because I never have until now."

"You were the little boy with the mean lady in the big red car?" Sherri asked, wide-eyed. "I always wondered who it was that day. Paw-Paw said it was just more looky-loos."

"You got a lot of those, did you?" he asked with a raised brow.

"I remember a few," she said. "Paw-Paw always said it was because our house was the highest point in the county, and he thought it had been a civil war outpost or something." Sherri shrugged her shoulders. "I guess it was something else, huh?"

"Yah," he said, "the house of the last man hung in the state."

"And now it's mine," she sighed.

Dylan reached over, took her hand, and smiled. "Might be a book in there somewhere." He shrugged. "You never know."

Sherri thought back on her experiences in the house and returned his grin. "Yep, you never know."

He pulled her close, bent, and kissed her. His lips were warm on hers as he pressed urgently with his tongue.

I think he wants this as much as I do, but not in the damned car this time.

Sherri pulled back when his fingers found her nipple. "You want to take this inside?"

"Console killing the mood?" he asked with a grin.

"Yah, sorta," she said with a giggle. "I'm not as limber as I used to be." She straightened in the seat and unsnapped her seatbelt. "My bed is much more comfortable."

"I can't wait to find out." He released his seatbelt and opened the door.

I want this to be good for the both of us.

Sherri smiled when she saw the bulge in the front of his jeans as he walked around to get her door. He groaned with pleasure when she gave it a playful squeeze after he opened the car door and stepped close to help her out.

Such a gentleman. I wonder what he'd do if I unzipped him and gave it a kiss right here? He said he liked spontaneous. Let's see if that's true.

Sherri sat back down, pulled him toward her, and massaged the bulge in Dylan's jeans as he stood moaning softly. He flinched a little when her hand tugged at his zipper, but he soon fumbled with his belt and unbuttoned his jeans.

"Damn, woman," he sighed when Sherri pulled him closer and kissed the head of his throbbing erection. "You're full of surprises," he gasped.

"Oh, shit," he moaned when she slid it into her mouth and began lapping at the base of the big head with her tongue.

Sherri felt him begin to tremble and she smiled.

Yep, I'm full of surprises. How about you big fella?

"Keep that up and I'm gonna blow in your mouth before I get a chance to enjoy that pussy."

Well, we can't have that. Can we?

Sherri pulled back but gave his erection one final tickle with her tongue. She stood and smiled up at Dylan. "My pussy is in need of a little enjoying."

"Awesome," he said and pulled her into his arms again for a long, ardent kiss.

Glad to know he's not one of those jerks who won't kiss a girl after she's had his dick in her mouth.

Sherri unlocked the door and they stumbled inside. Sherri kicked off her boots halfway across the living room as she shrugged out of her jacket and tossed it on the couch.

"Damn, that's sexy," Dylan sighed as he stared at her standing barefoot in the tight, strapless bustier and jeans.

He'd already taken off his shirt and stood with his muscular chest bare, his jeans open, and his hard erection at the ready. Sherri took a deep breath and tried to ignore the throbbing wetness between her thighs.

It's been too damned long.

Her last relationship had been over a year ago with a truck driver she'd met through an internet dating site. He'd been handsome and exciting, taking her to clubs she'd never been to.

It had been fun but ended when he decided to marry a lab technician in Phoenix he'd also met on the site. It had hurt and she'd sworn off men for a long time. She had cancelled her subscription to the dating site and refused to get involved with any men other than the ones in her books. It had been a long time since she'd desired a man.

Too damned long, but can I take that kind of hurt again?

Sherri began to pop the hooks on the bustier one at a time until her heavy breasts fell out. She backed into the dark bedroom and crooked her finger to beckon him. "Get in here and I'll show you sexy."

This is going to be fun.

❧ 18 ❧

Pounding at the door woke Sherri and she rolled over to peek at the clock by her bed.

Damn, it's almost seven and the guys are here.

She shook Dylan's shoulder. "Wake up, Dylan. Jeremy and the guys are here."

"What?" He yelped as he bolted up into a sitting position in the jumbled bed. "Damnit," he groaned as the pounding resumed, "I should have been out of here hours ago."

Sherri grinned and kissed his stubbled cheek. "You were busy hours ago."

"I was," he said and rolled from the bed to find his discarded jeans, "but this looks bad and very un-professional."

What is he talking about?

"Good lord," she sighed as she yanked her robe from the bedpost and put it on. "We're two adults not a couple of kids."

"But you're my client, Sherri. We shouldn't have done this." He fumbled with his belt as he tried to hurry things along.

You mean we shouldn't have gotten caught doing this by your crew.

"Which time?" Sherri snapped as she strode across the living room to open the door and let the men inside.

"Wake you up again, Sherri?" Jeremy said with a grin on his young face. "Ain't that the boss' car out there?"

Sherri picked up Dylan's discarded shirt and vest. She tossed them to him in the bedroom where he sat with a look of shame on his face that made her want to scream. "Yah," Sherri snarled as she padded into the kitchen to make coffee, "you woke him up too."

She heard good-natured chuckles amongst the men and then silence. Dylan strode to the bathroom without acknowledging her and slammed the door.

Is he really that ashamed of being caught together? It's fucking high school all over again. He's the campus bigshot and got caught having fun with the school tramp by his friends. Fuck this shit.

Sherri pushed past the grinning men, stormed to her bedroom with tears stinging her eyes, and slammed the door behind her. She buried her face in her pillow and sobbed.

Someone rapped on the door. Sherri sat up and wiped her face as Dylan stepped inside and closed the door.

"I'm sorry, Sherri," he said without meeting her eyes. "This was a mistake and should never have happened between us."

"Just go, Dylan," Sherri said and tried to hold back the tears.

"The project is nearly complete," he continued. "I'll leave Jeremy in charge to finish things up."

Just gonna bump and run, huh? It figures. You're just the same gutless ass you always were. You haven't changed.

"Get the hell out of my fucking house, Dylan," she screamed and tossed the sodden pillow at Dylan who opened the bedroom door and hopped out before she could find something more substantial to throw.

Sherri sank back down into the bed and sobbed. How could she have gone from blissfully happy to this in such a short time? After an hour, she heard a soft knock.

"Come in," she said and sat up, pulling her robe tight over her breasts.

Jeremy came in carrying a cup of steaming coffee. "Thought you might need this," he said and handed Sherri the cup.

"Thanks," she said softly and took the coffee he offered.

"The furnace guys are here. I showed 'em where to get started, but it's probably gonna get noisy with them walkin' around up in the loft hangin' that ductwork and all. The ceiling crew will be up there finishing today too." He patted her shoulder. "I think it's gonna look okay. The duct work they use is painted brown and not all shiny and galvanized like some."

"That's good," she said with a forced smile. "What's your crew working on today?"

"We have two more windows to install and the outside doors," he said, "and then the new inside doors. Ben and Mel are starting on the shutters today too."

"Sounds like it's gonna be a busy day," she said and took a sip of her coffee. "How long did the heat pump guys say they'd be?"

Jeremy shrugged. "Usually takes 'em a couple of days. We've done jobs like this with 'em before."

Sherri glanced down at the discolored floorboards and sighed, remembering Molly's pleading voice as she begged to be given a proper burial.

I know I promised, Molly, but I'm afraid to look.

Jeremy left the room and Sherri got up and dressed. In the living room, she retrieved her jacket and boots to return to her closet.

Well, it was fun, but it's over now. Never should have started in the first place. Like Dylan said, it never should have happened. I was such a fool.

"The boss never said what you wanted to do with these walls, Sherri," Jeremy said, staring up at the brown spots on the old wallpaper again. "I need to know before we can put the finish work on the windows."

"Take it all down to the logs," she sighed. "Not much sense having a log cabin if you can't see the damned logs."

"All of it?" He asked with his face screwed up in confusion. "It's probably gonna cost you more."

Sherri smiled at the young man. "It's your project now. Call Bobby and get the revised numbers for stripping this old plaster and staining the logs. This project belongs to you now. Make it yours, Jeremy."

"Yes, ma'am," he said eagerly and took out his phone.

I hope the kid gets credit for the whole damned job. I think I'll send an email to Bobby about it.

Jeremy came back, looking sheepish. "Bobby says it's gonna be another ten grand."

"No problem," Sherri said. "I'll give you a check to take back to the office this afternoon."

"Thanks, Sherri," he said with a relieved sigh. "I'll get some of the guys on it right away."

She slipped on a sweater, picked up her laptop, and went out to enjoy the sunny afternoon in the swing. In the drive were the trucks she recognized along with two white vans. Garrett Plumbing and Heating was emblazoned on the sides.

Oh, surely not.

Sherri put men out of her mind and concentrated on rewriting the first few chapters, incorporating some of the changes Inga had suggested after speaking with the editor at the publishing company. Sherri didn't like to work that way, but for the money they'd agreed to pay, she thought she could bend a little.

She was on a roll when another truck pulled into the drive and didn't look up from her work.

"Writing another of your sex-filled, trashy books, Sherri?" someone asked.

She looked up from her laptop to see Tommy Garrett standing over her with a notebook in his hand.

Really not what I need today.

"As a matter of fact, I am," she said and stared at the screen. "I didn't know you were in the furnace business, Tommy."

"It's just Tom now. I took over Uncle Gene's business when he retired a few years back," he said and licked his lips. "You're looking good, Sherri. I thought I was gonna cum in my shorts last night at Applebee's." He rubbed his crotch and grinned. "Have you given any thought to us getting together for a little fun?"

Yah, I've been thinking real hard about how it's never gonna happen.

"You're still very married, Tommy, so no, I haven't given it any thought at all."

The door burst open and Jeremy rushed out carrying her ringing phone. "I thought this might be important," he said and handed her the phone. "Oh, hey, Mr. Garrett, the guys are comin' along just fine in there."

Thank you, Jeremy. I owe you one.

Sherri didn't recognize the number other than it was local. "Hello, this is Sherri Lambert."

"Hi, Sherri, this is Louis Cummings from the library."

"Oh, hi, Louis. What can I do for you?"

"You asked me about those missing women and Miles Tucker the last time we talked."

"Yes," she said with her interest piqued. "What did you find out?"

"Not much, I'm afraid," he sighed. "I went through everything I could find on Tucker, then everything on missing persons reported during the years he was active."

"And?" she asked with a sinking feeling in her gut.

"Evidently he was running with a woman named Maude Baker back in twenty-two who went missing. When questioned about her, Tucker said she'd run off with a man she met at a tavern. She was a known party-girl and it was dropped."

Maude Baker, huh? I suppose that would be Maudie.

"A few years later," Louis said, "the family of Tilly Threewit reported her missing and said she'd been spending time with Tucker."

"And I suppose she ran off with another man too?"

Louis snorted. "Exactly, though the authorities pressed him a little harder on that one. The Three-wits were a pretty prosperous farm family back then."

"Is it the same family with the produce market in town?" Sherri asked, remembering going into the old shed market with her grandfather for nuts and citrus during the Christmas season.

"It is," he said. "They offered a big reward for news of the girl, but nothing ever came of it." He paused before going on. "This last girl I'm very familiar with."

"Tilly?"

"No," he said in a soft voice, "Molly—Molly Cummings. She was my grandfather's cousin and went missing in twenty-seven."

"Oh, my," Sherri said, "what was her story?"

Louis cleared his throat. "It was during Prohibition," he said, "and Tucker was several years older than Molly, but he was a bootlegger and had money."

"Just like young girls and gangbangers with money from selling drugs today. She was probably impressed with his money and he wasn't an ugly man, either."

Maybe I shouldn't have mentioned that. How would I know? All the pictures I saw were pretty poor.

"I couldn't speak to that," Louis huffed, "but she went missing after Tucker dragged her out of a tavern where she'd just chatted with my grandfather." She heard Louis take a deep breath.

"Until the day my grandfather died, he swore Tucker did something to Molly and it broke his heart that they hung the bastard before they could get any answers out of him."

"She was just another party-girl who hooked up with the wrong sort of man and the authorities couldn't give a damn," Sherri sighed.

"Something like that," Louis said. "I hope that helps. It's all I could find.

"Thanks, Louis. It was a big help. I'm putting some notes together for a future book on Tucker. I may want to get together sometime and get copies of everything you have on him and the missing women. I think that would be a good angle for the story."

"Wow," he said. "That would be amazing. There

has only been the one book written about him and they left a lot out. I think it's time for another." He took a breath. "I heard rumors flying around town that you're putting our little town on television. Is that true?"

Candi sure spread that bit of bullshit around Barrett pretty fast.

Sherri chuckled. "My agent has been shopping my books around to some producers," she said, "but nothing is firmed up yet."

"I was in the bookstore today and Jill told me they're sold out of your stuff. You should give her a call or drop some off. It sounds like they're selling like hot cakes."

"Thanks, Louis. I'll give Jill a call." She disconnected the call and threw her head back, laughing.

Oh, my lord. Maybe I should start some more rumors. Better yet, let Candi start some. She's got to be the cheapest damned publicist out there.

❀ 19 ❀

With all the turmoil in the house, Sherri spent most of the remainder of the work week out on the porch with her laptop. She finished rewriting the three chapters, sent them off to Inga, and revised her outline of all three books.

I think I can see this going places. It's been fun so far.

After speaking with Louis, she checked her phone messages and found a call from the bookstore requesting more books and another signing. She immediately ordered more copies, called the store, and set up a signing for the following Friday, the day after Thanksgiving and the busiest shopping day of the year.

On Friday, she got a call from Inga. "You're not gonna believe this," her agent gasped.

"What?" Sherri asked, sensing Inga's excitement.

"I just got a call from the people at the CW. They want to buy the rights to that little book you self-published—Lost Hope. Can you believe it? They think it will make a great addition to their teen-oriented line-up next season."

You have got to be shitting me.

"Wow," she said, trying to sound excited. "How much?"

"I'm still negotiating," she said, "but more than I would have thought. Your name's getting around out there, kid. I see big money in our futures. I'm shopping the Westerns to HBO and Showtime now and they both sound very interested now that the CW is picking you up.

Oh, wow. Wouldn't that be a kick in the ass? My books on HBO? Move over George R.R., Whiskey Treat is moving in on your turf.

"That's great, Inga. Keep me informed."

"You might want to think about a follow up to that Lost Hope novel. They'll want fodder for at least three seasons. I'm sure their writers will be in touch if we sign."

"I'll give it some serious thought. Thanks, Inga," Sherri said and disconnected.

I can't believe this. Maybe I should call Dylan and tell him thank you.

Dylan hadn't been back to the house or called. She hated to admit it, but she missed him terribly. Jeremy said he thought Dylan had gone back to Mississippi to visit his daughter and grandson.

It's just as well. It looks like I should be focusing on my career now anyway.

One of the things Jeremy had taken upon himself to do was put in the stone wall she wanted in the kitchen and it looked fabulous. The new heat pump warmed the house and Sherri had purchased new curtains and rugs. As the kitchen stove hadn't arrived yet, she was still living on toasted bagels and microwaved meals. Hopefully, that would be over next week, and she'd have new cabinets too.

The place looks great. I wish Dylan was here to see the progress.

Over the weekend, Sherri enjoyed the quiet, caught up on laundry, and curled up on the couch with her laptop for some serious writing time. Her eyes began to droop, and she set the computer aside and closed them.

I haven't been able to take a nap in weeks. No time like the present, I suppose.

The odor of cigarettes woke her, and Sherri opened her eyes in a dark room. Across from her on the loveseat sat a man with a cigarette dangling from his lips. She inched herself up into a sitting position.

"I like what you've done with the place, Doll," he said, "but you need some ashtrays. It's a shame to mess up these nice floors with ashes and butts."

"Miles?" Sherry asked. "What are you doing here? You didn't die here, and you had a proper burial, so what are you doing *here*?"

He snorted, took the cigarette from his mouth, and tapped the ashes to fall onto the floor. "It weren't no proper funeral with a preacher. They just put me in an old pine box after they stretched my neck and buried me in an unmarked grave in the city cemetery. I'm free to come visit my girls now and again if I want to," he said with a deep chuckle that reminded Sherri of Dylan.

"I've visited you too," he said with a smile as he squeezed his crotch. "Wanna give me a little of that sweet stuff now or are you savin' it for that fool nephew of mine?"

"I'm not giving anything to either one of you. You're both a couple of pigs, but at least Dylan never murdered anyone."

Miles was suddenly beside Sherri on the couch. "Oh, come on, Doll," he said and put a very firm hand on her breast, "You know you like it. You've always liked it."

Oh, my lord. I'm an asshole magnet. It doesn't matter if they're living or dead.

"Leave the gal alone, Daddy," said a soft female voice.

Both their heads jerked up to see Molly standing at the end of the couch in her shimmering blue dress. "Molly Doll," Miles breathed and pushed Sherri aside. "I've missed you, Doll," he said and rushed into her outstretched arms.

"I've missed you too, Daddy," Molly said and rolled her eyes at Sherri. "Let's go in here and play for a while." She smiled at the man, led Miles into the bedroom, and the door closed behind them.

Oh, great. I hope pecker tracks from a dead guy come out of the sheets.

"This has got to end soon, Doll," another female voice hissed.

Sherri glanced over at the loveseat to see Tilly and Maude had joined her. "I know," Sherri said, "and it will."

Both women sipped clear liquid from tall glasses with lime slices wedged on the rims.

I could use a gin and tonic about now or a strong shot of Jack Daniels. I gotta get some the next time I'm in town.

"Tilly," Sherri said in a hushed voice, "I know who your family is, and I promised Molly I'd see to getting your bodies to your families for a proper burial." Her eyes moved to the other woman. "I don't know who your family is, though, Maude. Where should I go to look for them? Did you have brothers and sisters? Cousins?"

Maude shook her head. "All my kin are dead and waitin' for me to cross over," she said sadly, "but we hailed from Upton. My pops was dead when I ran off with Miles and my mom not long after. I had a brother," she sighed, "but he died in a mine collapse in nineteen twenty-two. I guess there's nobody left to pay for words to be said over me." A tear slid down her pale cheek.

"Don't worry," Sherri promised, "you'll have words said over you and have the biggest funeral this county's ever seen."

"You think?" she said excitedly. "I'd like a pretty white coffin with a soft satin lining. I've been lying on the cold, hard ground for too long. I'd like to rest in some comfort now."

Sherri smiled. "I think we can manage that."

Her phone sounded with a text message and startled Sherri. She rummaged through papers on the coffee table until she found her phone and picked it up.

The message was from Dylan and her finger hovered over the glass as she decided if she wanted to open it or not. She finally took a deep breath and opened the text. Sherri glanced at the love seat, but the women were gone.

DR: I guess ur still mad at me.

Are you kidding? Of course, I'm still mad.

SL: I am.

DR: OK

OK? Just OK? Well, OK then. I'm so done with this bullshit.

Sherri waited for another text, but when none came, she tossed the phone back on the table and curled up on the couch again. She let the tears flow for a while, then got up and took a hot shower.

She loved the new bathroom and had found a

frilly lace curtain to hang around the tub with one to match at the window. A can of robin's egg-blue paint sat in the corner to go on the walls as soon as the bead board wainscot and moldings were installed.

This is the house I grew up in, but it's different now. I'm making it mine. It's not my grandparents' house anymore and it's not Miles Tucker's house. It's my house.

❦ 20 ❦

When Jeremy and the crew arrived on Monday morning. Sherri was waiting for them in the kitchen with coffee and a large box of donuts.

"Donuts?" Jeremy said with a raised brow. "What's up?" He took a jelly donut from the box. "What project do you have for us now?"

"I've been giving a lot of thought to that blood on the wall in there and the stain on the floor beneath it," she said to Jeremy the crime junkie.

"And?" he asked with a raised brow as he took a cup of coffee from her hand.

Sherri took a deep breath. "And," she said, "I want you to pull up that floor up in the bedroom to see what's under there. It's been bugging me, and I have to know what's down there."

"Yes!" he yelled and threw his fist into the air triumphantly. "I knew you'd see it my way."

The other men groaned and shook their heads. "You shouldn't encourage him, Sherri. He already thinks he's Sherlock Holmes or something."

"Just shut up, Mel," Jeremy said with a pout on his face. "Sherri understands. She sees the clues and can put two and two together just like me."

I've seen a few more clues, though.

"Sherri is a writer," Mel said as he grabbed his second donut. "She gets paid to make somethin' outta nothin'."

"This ain't nothin'," Jeremy snapped. "Something bad happened here. The blood on that wall in there proved it."

"You don't even know if that was blood, boy," Mel said with a chuckle. "Some kid probably splashed his chocolate milk on the wall."

All the men laughed except Jeremy, and Sherri felt sorry for him, but she knew he'd be redeemed when that floor came up.

Just hang in there, kid. You'll be able to make them eat their words later.

He emptied his cup with a scowl on his young face. "Let's get to it," Jeremy said and pushed away from the table. "How much do you want us to take up?" He asked Sherri.

"I think you should probably take up that whole mismatched section," she said and saw Mel roll his eyes.

Sherri had already moved the bed aside and picked up the rugs to reveal the cracked and splintered floorboards. "Do you think you can pull them up without doing too much more damage to them?" She asked.

"We've got plenty of stuff we can replace it with back at the warehouse," Jeremy said, "but we'll be careful with it anyway."

"Thanks," she told him before returning to the kitchen to straighten things up. She moved her laptop to the kitchen and waited.

Jeremy received more ribbing and Sherri smiled as she listened to the good-natured banter coming from her bedroom.

"Jesus, Mary, and Joseph," she heard Mel call out and knew they'd found something.

Sherri got to her feet and rushed toward the bedroom. She met a very pale Benny in the living room. "What is it?" She asked.

"You better call the Sheriff, ma'am," he mumbled, "there's a skeleton down there."

More than one, if I'm not mistaken. I'm glad Jeremy has been redeemed, though.

Benny hurried outside where he hung onto a porch post and emptied his stomach into the bed of the mums. Sherri stepped into the bedroom to see the other four men bent over a hole in the floor. One held the lamp from her bedside table over the opening and another held a flashlight.

"What did you find?" Sherri asked in a soft voice as she joined them.

"It's a fucking body," Jeremy said with a look on his face somewhere between joy and terror. "A woman, I think. That looks like a dress of some kind."

In the hole, Sherri saw yellowed bones draped in a garment she couldn't recognize. Bits of dried skin and brown hair clung to a grinning skull.

Maude or Tilly. Molly was wearing blue and her hair was blonde not brown.

"I suppose you'd better take the rest of it up," she said with her hand at her chest. "I'll call the Sheriff."

By the time a sheriff's deputy arrived, Jeremy had uncovered the remains of two more women and Sherri knew one of them was Molly.

Around the decomposed body, Sherri saw remnants of blue cloth and scattered about were blue beads and ragged bits of fringe. A few clumps of blonde curls still clung to the small yellowed skull.

The blood on her dress must have attracted mice and rats that made a meal of it over time and scattered the beads.

"Is this the location of the bodies?" A potbellied deputy asked after he lumbered to the door, stinking of cigarettes.

"Yes," Sherri said and showed him into the bedroom where they'd set up more lights.

"All y'all are gonna have to get out of here," the deputy growled. "You're tramplin' the crime scene."

"Mister," Jeremy sneered and pointed down into the opening in the floor, "this hasn't been a crime scene for several decades. These bodies have been down here for years."

The portly deputy tramped over and peered down into the hole where three skulls grinned up at him. "Oh, my lord," he muttered and stumbled back. "I'm … eh … I'm gonna call this in and get the coroner out here." He rushed from the house to his patrol car.

"There's some high-quality law enforcement there," Jeremy said with a chuckle. "Probably couldn't find his way out of a bag of donuts with neon arrows pointing the way."

"Looks like he was too busy stoppin' to eat 'em," Benny said, and everyone laughed.

Jeremy snorted in agreement. "I wouldn't trust that asshole with any crime scene."

An hour later, the coroner's van and two more county police vehicles sat in her drive with their lights flashing.

"I'm Detective Summary," a medium height man with neatly trimmed hair that had once been red, but was now salted liberally with silver, said to Sherri as he extended his hand.

"Mack Summary?" she asked with a smile as she took his hand. "Sherri Lambert."

Mack had been a grade ahead of her at Barrett High and had married a girl from near her house. They'd attended the same small elementary school.

"Yah," he said and returned her smile. "I heard you were back in the area and a writer for television or something." He looked toward the brightly lit bedroom. "What's going on here? I heard you found some bodies under your floor?"

"This was my grandparents' place and I've been renovating it," she said and swept her hand around the house. "We noticed some odd things and I had the guys take up a bit of floor in the bedroom. We found skeletons and called the Sheriff's office."

Mack took out a notebook and began scribbling notes. "What sort of odd things?"

"Let me get Jeremy, my foreman in here. He's the real crime buff and put it together before anyone else." She called for the lanky young man to join them.

"Yah, Sherri?" he asked as he came into the living room.

"Jeremy, this is Detective Summary and he'd like to ask you some questions about what you found."

"Sure," the young man said and stood a little straighter as he took the Detective's hand. "What do you want to know?"

"Ms. Lambert said you noticed some things unusual that lead to this discovery?"

He looks like a little boy who just found a pirate treasure in his back yard,

Jeremy's eyes flitted to Sherri with the shadow of a grateful grin before answering the Detective's question. "Well, first off when we redid the floors, we found this spot here that looked to me like an obvious blood pool around a sitting body." He led the detective to the spot on the floor and pointed. "Then we found blood spatter on some old wallpaper when we started stripping the walls to replace the windows." He took out his phone and showed Mack the many photos he'd taken.

This makes all the guys' bullshitting worth it. The kid is having a field day with this. He deserves it.

As day turned to night and the coroner's van pulled away with the remains of the three women arranged on cotton batting in flat plastic containers. Sherri stared around her quiet, but disheveled house and sighed.

I hope this puts an end to the spectral visitations. I can really use the rest. Maybe I should go to the animal shelter and get a cat. I've heard they are sensitive to ghosts and the like.

As her bedroom had a huge hole in the floor and smelled vaguely of the grave, Sherri elected to sleep on the couch. Jeremy had promised to put the floor back in order tomorrow with new boards from the Realistic Renovations warehouse. He promised to sand and seal them as well.

Dylan didn't text or call and that made her sad, but she sucked it up. If he called, he called, and if he didn't, he didn't. She'd gotten by all these years without him. She would get by now.

❦ 21 ❦

The days leading up to Thanksgiving were a blur. The news media got wind of the story and news vans replaced the coroner's vans in Sherri's driveway. Jeremy repeated his sleuthing techniques, and Sherri was happy to share the spotlight with the young man.

They were both featured on local television news reports and in the area's major newspapers. Inga texted her that the story had been picked up by the AP and had made it to papers in New York, LA, and USA Today.

The books she'd ordered for the signing on Friday arrived and Sherri packed them into the rear of the PT. She hoped for a busy day and good sales.

Inga says no news is bad news when it comes to publicity. I hope that is true, but I'm ready for some peace and quiet for a while around here.

The cabinets arrived and were installed along with black granite countertops and the antique stove. Sherri was glad to see the old cabinets added to the burn pile out back.

While the guys replaced her floor and stained the

logs a rich reddish brown in the rest of the house, Sherri painted the bathroom. The soft blue on the walls against the bright white fixtures and wainscot looked heavenly and Sherri was happy with the results.

As she slid a turkey into the oven, it began to snow and by the time she took the bird out with brown, crispy skin, five inches of the white stuff had accumulated in the yard. She texted Bobby that he should send out his photographer. They might not get snow again until after Christmas.

He texted back and said he would. He also thanked her for mentioning the company and how much she loved the renovation in all the press coverage.

No publicity is bad publicity.

Sherri sliced some dark meat from the thigh, smeared mayo on both slices of soft, white bread, and returned to the couch with her sandwich, some chips, and a tall glass of root beer over ice.

Some Thanksgiving dinner. Maybe next year when I'm not dealing with ghosts haunting my dreams, dead bodies in my crawlspace, and a complete renovation of my house. Who am I kidding? I don't have anybody to cook for but me and turkey sandwiches are just fine by me.

Her phone chimed with a text. When she saw Realistic Renovation's number on the screen, she expected it to be a message from Bobby about the photographer.

RR: How is your Thanksgiving? This is Dylan. I hear you've been busy.

SL: That's putting it mildly. Where are you? Mississippi?

RR: Got back this morning. Carla Jean and Kyle went to the Gulf with friends. What are you doing?

SL: Eating a turkey sandwich and missing you.

I might as well be honest.

RR: I can fix that.

SL: If you don't mind turkey sandwiches.

RR: I'll bring the wine.

SL: Chardonnay?

RR: You got it. See you in a few. I can't wait to see the finished product. I've missed you too.

Sherri stared down at her paint-stained jeans and old sweater.

I'm not dressing up for him. He probably wouldn't appreciate it anyhow. I am what I am, and he'll have to deal with that.

The house smelled like roast turkey with an undertone of fresh paint. She added a log to the fire and smiled up at the deer head she'd had mounted above the dark mantle Jeremy had fashioned from an old railroad tie.

It looked just like the fireplace from her vision and Sherri liked it. The painting of the old cabin hung over the couch and the antique hurricane lamps changed to electric graced the end tables. Gingham curtains hung at the windows and patchwork throws draped the backs of the couch and loveseat Sherri couldn't bear to part with.

Sherri straightened rugs throughout the house

and fluffed the pillows on her bed. In the kitchen, she set out two wine glasses and put together a tray with sliced turkey, cheddar cheese, grapes, and Ritz Crackers.

That's gonna have to do.

She heard his truck pull up and carried the tray of snacks and wine glasses to the coffee table. Sherri was at the door when he knocked. She opened the door and his smile took her breath away for a moment as her heart began to pound in her chest.

I bet my damned cheeks have turned red like a damned teenager's.

"Hi," she said as she pushed open the screen door. "Did you have any trouble getting up the hill in the snow?"

Dylan smiled and glanced at his big red pickup. "It's four-wheel drive and I have the rear end full of pecan logs I brought back from Mississippi for my smoker."

He stepped inside with a bottle of wine in one hand and a bouquet of roses in the other. Dylan stomped the snow off his boots on the oval braided rug and handed Sherri the flowers.

Wine and flowers, huh? Typical man.

"I figured I owed you after the last time I was here."

That's about the lamest apology I've ever heard.

Sherri took the flowers and closed the door. "Come on in the kitchen. I have a bottle opener. You can do the honors while I put these in water," she said and lifted the bouquet of roses to her nose.

Dylan stared around the room and up into the loft. "The place looks great," he said as he walked to the fireplace. He reached up and petted the deer head. "I like this. It's a nice touch."

If you only knew where I got the idea.

"Thanks," she said and went into the kitchen. Dylan followed.

He stopped in front of the stove and whistled. "This is perfect and the stone behind it was an excellent idea."

Sherri took a clear vase from beneath the new Irish farm sink, filled it with water, and arranged the roses. She set them on the round table beneath the 70s era fixture, hanging from the rafters by a coppertone chain.

"This came together great," he said, "and you were absolutely right about boxing in the refrigerator with those tall pantry cabinets. I'm gonna have to keep that in mind for the next job."

"Thanks," she said. "I saw it in Country Living once and liked it for use with a modern refrigerator. How's your grandson?"

Dylan opened the door and peeked into the small bedroom Sherri had furnished with a twin bed, dresser, and nightstand in knotty pine.

"He's great," Dylan said. "Looking forward to a long weekend at the beach."

"Must be nice," Sherri sighed as she fiddled nervously with the roses.

"Hey, you're a rich woman now with book and television deals. You could go to the coast anytime you wanted."

"Yah, right," she snorted and rolled her eyes. "I suppose I should cut you a commission on that television thing."

"I beg your pardon?" he said as he picked up the wine and carried it to the couch.

Sherri joined him. "You told Candi that night that I'd been offered a deal on Lost Hope from the CW."

"Yah," he said with a grin. "I was fucking with

her and it worked. I could always push her fucking buttons."

"I know you were fucking with her, but Candi didn't and she, along with a bunch of her friends, called the producers and raised holy hell. They swore they'd sue if the CW turned Lost Hope into a series."

Sherri giggled as she poured wine into their glasses. "The producer, of course, didn't know what the hell they were talking about and got curious, read the book, and thought it would make a great addition to their line-up."

"Are you shitting me?" Dylan said with a broad grin and asked with a twinkle in his brown eyes. "How much exactly would my cut be?"

"My agent got about twenty-grand out of the deal and she didn't do shit," Sherri said with a giggle, "so I guess you deserve at least that much."

Dylan's eyes went wide. "You've got to be kidding."

"Want me to write you a check?" she asked with a grin and nibbled on a salty cracker loaded up with turkey and cheddar.

Dylan exhaled a long sigh. "I could certainly use the cash, but that's all right. I'll get by."

Louis said the company might be in trouble. I wonder what's up.

Sherri thought for a minute before reaching into her purse for her checkbook. "I can write it off my taxes as a business expense," she said as she wrote out a check to Dylan for twenty-thousand dollars. "Bobby already got me for another ten."

"What the hell for?" he snapped and ignored the check she pushed in front of him.

"I decided I wanted all the walls taken down to the logs," she said and pointed to the log wall behind the couch, "not just the end walls and he said it would be an extra ten-grand in labor."

Dylan shook his head as he bit into a square of cheese. "That greedy son-of-a-bitch," he hissed as he chewed. "That was already in the bid price. Keep that," he said and pushed her check back to her on the coffee table. "and I'll get your other ten back from Bobby."

Sherri grabbed Dylan's hand and put the check into it. "Take this," she said with a grin. "You earned it, and like I said before, it comes right off the top of my taxes and my accountant says I'm gonna need all the write-offs I can get this year because of the new book deal and now this television thing."

"You have a fucking accountant?" He sighed, picked up a handful of grapes from the tray, and bit into one.

She took a long swallow of the sweet wine and smiled at Dylan staring at the check in his hand. "And don't get into a fuss with Bobby over this. I think Jeremy knew he was trying to take advantage of me, and he did a lot of extra things around here for me. I'm very happy with how it's all turned out."

She glanced around the warm, inviting room and smiled. "It's beautiful and I couldn't have asked for more."

Dylan folded the check and slid it into his shirt pocket. "Thanks, Sherri. I really appreciate it." He smiled. "Kyle wants a damned motorcycle for Christmas and Carla Jean could use some help with a new car. Her old Volvo is on its last leg."

"Are things not going well with the business?" She asked and refilled their glasses.

"The business is fine," Dylan sighed. "It's Bobby. I didn't know it before we started this business together, but he has a gambling problem." He popped a cracker with turkey and cheese into his mouth followed with some wine.

"Oh, I see," she said.

I guess Molly was wrong and Bobby ended up with the bad Tucker blood; not Dylan.

"He visits the gambling boats down on the river every chance he gets or flies out to Vegas." Dylan took a deep breath. "I didn't know it, but the gambling is what ended his marriage and it's about to end our business partnership. I've only been keeping it together because of my mom. She refuses to admit he has a damned problem, though he's almost drained her savings."

Sherri put a hand on his. "I'm sorry to hear that, Dylan. It seems like a good business."

"It is," he said, "but Bobby keeps pissing everything away and I can't afford to cover his debts any longer."

Damn, this really seems to have him down.

Sherri scooted closer, took his face in her hands, and kissed him. He wrapped his arms around her and pulled her into his body.

"I need you, Sherri," he whispered. "I'm sorry I was such an ass. It'll never happen again. I should have been here with you when they pulled up that floor and found those bodies. It must have been horrible."

She pushed back and smiled up at Dylan. "It probably wouldn't have happened if you'd been here. I had them pull up the floor because I was still pissed at you."

Well, that was part of the reason, anyway.

Dylan returned her smile. "Oh, I see. Well, you certainly made Jeremy's day. He's talking about enrolling in a criminal justice program and joining the Sheriff's Department."

Sherri chuckled. "I suppose finding dead bodies under the floor of a house you're working on is better than playing Cold Case on the computer."

"He didn't mind all the media attention either."

"Or the fact that he got to tell the guys I told you so, after all the bullshit they gave him about his theories." Sherri emptied her glass of wine. "That had better be my last one," she said. "I have a book signing in town tomorrow and don't want to show up with a pounding head."

"You should wear something sexy," he said and kissed her again. "Would my spending the night throw you off your game too much?"

Watch it Lambert. Remember how it turned out the last time he spent the night.

Sherri leaned into his kiss.

Oh, what the hell.

"Not in the least," she whispered and took his hand to lead him into the bedroom.

❧ 22 ❧

Sherri woke in her dark room with Dylan pressed against her back, kissing her neck and his erect penis pressed between the back of her thighs.

Doesn't this man ever wear out? We've been at it all night.

"You awake?" he asked when he felt her move.

"I am now," she said groggily into her pillow.

"Good," Dylan said as he pushed into her throbbing pussy from behind, "because so am I."

Yah, I get that.

He reached over and pinched Sherri's nipple as he pumped into her. She met him thrust for thrust and they climaxed together, matching groans of pleasure upon the disheveled bed.

Dylan rolled onto his back, panting. "Damn, woman, you know how to make a man happy in bed."

Sherri grabbed a tissue and stuffed it between her legs before sitting up and throwing her legs off the mattress. "You haven't tasted my fabulous cooking yet. I know how to make a man happy in the kitchen too," she said and slapped his bare ass playfully. "I wish I didn't have to get up and do this signing today. I'd much rather spend the day here in bed with you."

He reached for her. "Can you cancel? I'd love you to cook me something."

"That would be very unprofessional," she chided, using his own words. "Anyway, the back of my car is full of books and today is the biggest shopping day of the year." She walked toward the door. "I'll have coffee ready in a few."

Sherri put on a pot of coffee and then jumped in the shower to wash the remnants of the frisky night away.

Damn, that was fun, but I'm gonna keep it in perspective. It's just fun between two adults—friends with benefits. Very nice benefits, though.

Sherri stepped out of the shower, toweled off, giving her hair some extra attention, and moussed her curls, hoping to keep them in place for the busy day ahead.

I hope it dries a little before I have to go out into this cold. I need to leave early too. I don't want to take any chances in this snow. They don't have snow in Palm Springs. I'm out of practice.

When she came out of the bedroom, Dylan was sitting at the table naked with two cups of coffee poured.

"Thanks, sweetie," she said and took a sip of the strong, hot brew. "That's just what I needed."

He snaked an arm around her waist. "I think the only thing I need is you, Sherri."

Oh, come on, Dylan. You're better than the cheesy morning-after bullshit. I write that crap and I hope you're not waiting for a sappy reply. It ain't gonna happen.

"Somehow, I doubt that," she said and took another swallow of the hot coffee.

Dylan grabbed her hand before she could walk away. "I mean it, Sherri. I think you're what's been missing in my life."

Sherri stood, gaping at him while he continued. "I've never had as much fun with a woman as I do with you. Even in high school, you could always make me laugh and I need that in my life."

But I was never good enough back then to ask out. I wasn't good enough for the Snot Squad. What makes it any different now?

Sherri put her hand up to stop him. "That's nice of you to say, Dylan, but I really think you should give this some thought. Things haven't changed that much in forty years. You're still a townie with a good name and I'm still just country trash."

"That's not true," he snapped. "You may live in the country, but you're certainly not trash." He grinned up at her. "Things have changed, Sherri. I'm just a working stiff now with money troubles because his little brother can't stay away from the damned crap tables and you're a famous author who is loaded."

"I'm not loaded," she scoffed and gulped more coffee.

"Bullshit," he snapped. "You did this total renovation without having to finance a dime and you wrote me a damned check for twenty-grand like you were paying for a couple boxes of Girl Scout Cookies."

Is it just the damned money? I have a few bucks in the bank, so now I qualify to be a member of the Snot Squad?

"All right," she sighed, "so I'm doing okay in the money department right now." She shrugged. "I'd rather you didn't spread that around, by the way."

Sherri walked back and kissed his cheek. "Let's just have some fun with this, Dylan, and see where it goes. Okay?" She emptied her coffee cup and turned back to the bedroom. "I gotta get ready for this thing."

"What time will you be done?"

"I think Jill said she's closing the store at seven tonight unless she's really busy. So, I guess I could be getting back here any time between eight and ten," Sherri said with a slight shrug and fled into the bedroom. "You still have a key, don't you?"

"Yah," he said as he pulled on his jeans. "Do you want it back?"

"No," she said as she put on a pair of stockings. "Keep it. You can let yourself in if you come back and I'm not back yet." She pulled on a black wool pencil skirt and zipped it.

His face lit up with a smile. "That's great. We can spend the weekend together and see if we can stand one another for more than a day."

The weekend, huh? Things must really be tense at home with Bobby if he wants to spend the weekend with me out here.

"That sounds great," Sherri said, returning his smile as she pulled a white camisole over her head and adjusted her breasts in the built-in bra. "I'll cook you a proper breakfast tomorrow morning."

"That sounds great. Do you need anything from the IGA?" he asked as he sat on the edge of the bed to put on his socks and boots. "I just came into some money and think I can afford some groceries."

Sherri smiled. "No, I think I have everything I need." She opened the closet and slipped into a pair of black leather flats as she pulled the wool jacket that went with the tight, sleek skirt from a hanger. "I went to the store on Tuesday just so I could get away from the noise and confusion around here. I had to make the funeral arrangements for Maude Baker too."

"When is that gonna be?" Dylan asked as he buttoned his shirt.

"It's gonna be on Sunday at Crider's," Sherri

said, "It took the Coroner longer than he thought to catalogue and reassemble the skeletons and get familial DNA matches for Tilly Threewit and Molly Cummings."

"Nobody came forward for Maude Baker?"

"No," Sherri sighed and shook her head, "so I took care of it. Her folks and brother were buried over in the churchyard near Upton and there was a plot available close by. She's going in the ground there beside them."

Dylan walked over and kissed Sherri's cheek as she applied some makeup. "You're a good woman, Sherri Lambert. Not many people would take on that kind of responsibility."

"She was under my house, so I felt kind of responsible for her."

I made a promise and I intend to keep it. Maudie will get words said over her so she can be released from this Earth to be with her family again.

"If Miles Tucker killed her," Dylan sighed, "then she's technically my responsibility and this house belonged to my family when she went under it. I should have been the one to pay for her damned funeral, not you."

"It didn't cost that much," she said and patted his hand on her shoulder, "and it's all taken care of." She took a deep breath. "How did your mom take all this when they started blaming the murders of the women on Miles Tucker?"

"Not good," he sighed and shook his head, "And Bobby is talking about forgoing the ad campaign with this house because of the negative publicity."

"I'm sorry to hear that. I wonder why he didn't mention it when I texted him about sending out a photographer yesterday to get pictures of the house with snow on the roof." Sherri sighed heavily. "I think you should all show up at the funerals so the media can see your family support."

"Are you going to go, then?"

You bet I am. I made promises to those girls.

"Me and hundreds of other people," she said. "The media has played it all up so much the funeral home said they've been swamped with calls about the services for the women. They're expecting a big crowd and I think all y'all should be there too."

Sherri stood. "I need to get going," she said. "I want to take it easy on the snowy blacktop, so I don't end up in a ditch. It's been years since I had to drive in more than rain and sandstorms."

"I'm gonna follow you in," Dylan said and kissed her again.

They left together and Dylan followed her all the way to the little bookstore on Barrett's main street. He even helped her carry in the books and other things for her signing table.

Dylan pointed at the poster of Sherri the bookstore had printed using the author photo from the back of her books and posted in the window to advertise the book signing. "You see," he said and smiled, "you're famous."

Sherri grinned. "Hardly," she said and gave him a quick kiss on the cheek. "I'll see you tonight when this is all over."

"You certainly will," he said, pulled her into his strong arms, and kissed her passionately on the mouth in the middle of the store. Sherri blushed when she saw the store employees staring with grins on their faces.

Well, that'll be all over town tomorrow.

The day passed in a flurry of chatting with old acquaintances, selling books, and signing. Sherri sold all their books through the store's register on the standard consignment split. It was the least she could do for Jill and she didn't have to deal with the sales tax and making change.

Louis stopped by with all his Tucker research and thanked her for returning Molly to the family.

"Will you be at the funeral?" he asked. "I heard they are going to stagger the graveside services so people can attend all three." He rolled his eyes behind his thick glasses. "It's turned into a really big deal here in Barrett."

Molly and the girls will like that—a big send-off after being lost and forgotten for so long.

"I definitely will. I wouldn't miss it," she said and shook his hand. "I'll study all of this and get back to you if I need anything else."

The only low point in the day was when Candi and her mother came into the store. Her mother was drunk and ripped down the poster of Sherri from the window while yelling vulgar slurs about the author and her books.

Candi marched to the table and pointed a finger at Sherri. "See what you've done."

"Not me," Sherri said as she signed another copy of Lost Hope, "I didn't buy her the bottle."

Those standing around the table and close by giggled. Candi's red face turned redder and she turned to stalk away.

"Are you gonna write a sequel to Lost Hope?" someone asked and Candi turned to glare at Sherri as she waited for the answer.

Sherri smiled sweetly at the former cheerleader who'd made her life miserable in high school. "As a matter of fact, I am," she said. "The network wants more in case they want to continue the series past the first three seasons they have planned." Sherri glanced at Candi who stood with her mouth agape. "I'll send your autographed copy to Pike's, Candi."

Karma's a bitch isn't she, Candi.

The woman grabbed her mother by the arm and dragged her from the busy store.

"I'm sorry about that," the store manager said, shaking her blonde head. "I can't believe Candi brings her out when she's in that condition."

"It's probably better than being cooped up in the house with her," Sherri sighed.

"It's been a great day, Sherri," Jill bent and whispered as she stared at the few remaining books on Sherri's table, "but I'm gonna need more books for the shelves."

"I'll leave you these," she said, "and place another order next week. I'm glad the store had a good day."

"Are you kidding?" Jill said with a broad smile. "I think it's going to be my best sales day ever." Jill gave Sherri a hug. "Maybe we can fit another in before Christmas?"

"Sounds like a plan," Sherri said. "Get with me in a week about a date."

As Sherri walked to her car, her phone chimed with a text. She pulled the phone from her purse when she got into the car and started the engine to warm up. She didn't recognize the local number but opened the text anyhow.

UN: This is Dylan. My phone is dead. Meet me for a drink at The Limits?

I didn't think he liked that place.

SL: Sure. Sounds good. Just got in the car.

UN: I'll be waiting.

I can use a drink after my day, but only one.

Sherri drove to the little bar on the edge of town and was glad to see the day's sun had melted the snow from the pavement. She turned into the parking lot and looked for Dylan's truck or the company car. When she didn't see either one, Sherri parked in an empty space near the end of the block building that was clear of snow.

I wonder if the battery on his truck died too.

With a smile on her face, Sherri grabbed her purse and opened the car door. The cold air took her breath away and she was happy for the warm, wool jacket.

"Nice of you to answer my invitation," someone said and grabbed her arm. "I saved this spot in the dark just for us, Sherri."

What the hell?

Sherri jerked her head up and stared up into the glazed eyes of Tommy Garrett. "What the hell are you talking about, Tommy," she hissed as she tried to wrench her arm from his grasp. "I'm here to meet Dylan."

"Settle down, Sherri," he growled and shook her. "Dylan's not coming. That text was from me." He pulled her into his arms and crushed his face into hers with an attempted kiss.

His breath reeks of stale alcohol and cigarettes. I think I'm gonna puke.

Tommy pushed her struggling body onto the hood of her car, pulled up her skirt, and shoved a hand between her legs. "I'm gonna screw you right here on your car, Sherri." He shoved fingers into her and grinned. "Your pussy is still tight. I like that."

"Let go of me asshole," she screamed and

brought her knee up for a violent thrust into Tommy's groin.

"Fucking cunt," Tommy yelled and drew his fisted hand for a punch, "I'm gonna fuck you in the ass for that and it's gonna hurt bad."

Not if you still have that little cock I remember.

Tears of rage and pain spilled from her eyes as she continued to struggle with Tommy Garrett on the hood of her car and she brought her knee up again with all her strength. She heard him gasp in pain and she smiled. The last thing Sherri saw that night was Tommy's fist as it crashed into her face.

❧ 23 ❧

"You need to wake up, Doll," Molly said as she ran a hand through Sherri's hair. "Wake up or we won't be able to say a proper goodbye."

Sherri stared up into Molly's bright, blue eyes. "What happened?"

"A silly man, of course," Molly sighed. "It's always a silly man."

"My head hurts," Sherri mumbled and tried to lift her hand.

"I bet it does. That bastard walloped you good, Doll." Molly smiled again. "Now wake up so you can come and tell us goodbye."

"Sherri?" She heard a familiar male voice. "Wake up, sweetheart. I'm here."

Sherri's eyes fluttered open and she saw Dylan sitting beside her, holding her hand.

"There you are," he said with a relieved smile as he brushed hair from her face. "You were talking in your sleep. You must have been dreaming."

"Molly," she muttered and tried to smile. "Molly was here and told me to wake up. She doesn't want me to miss the funeral."

Dylan smiled sadly. "The funeral is in the morning," he said. "I don't think the doctor will let you go."

For the first time, Sherri glanced around at her surroundings. "I'm in the hospital?"

"You don't remember what happened?" Dylan squeezed her hand. "The doctor said you might not. You have a concussion and a fractured jaw from where the bastard hit you."

"You texted me to come for a drink at The Limits."

Dylan frowned. "Not me, that ass wipe Garrett."

Sherri tried to lift her hand to her throbbing head. "Tommy," she mumbled, and tears filled her eyes, "Tommy hit me and he … he … Did he …?"

"No, he didn't do anything other than put his filthy hands on you and punch you in the head." Dylan smiled. "You gave the bastard a good one, though. He's in a room on the surgical floor. You ruptured one of his balls and they had to remove it." Dylan chuckled. "You very nearly made him castrati."

"Good," she whispered. "My head hurts."

"I'll go tell the nurse you're awake and need something for the pain."

Dylan left the room. Something whistled and beeped above her head, but Sherri couldn't see it. She lifted her hand and saw a needle stuck into her vein and taped down. A clear plastic tube ran from it a disappeared over her head.

I hate fucking hospitals. They smell bad and the food is terrible. I've got to get out of here. I can't miss their funerals.

Dylan returned with a nurse in tow. "How are you feeling, Ms. Lambert?" she asked as she pushed buttons on the monitor above Sherri's head.

"My head hurts and I need to pee," Sherri croaked through dry lips.

The woman in a Hello Kitty scrub top smiled. "You have a catheter in, so you don't really need to pee."

I hate fucking catheters too. I feel like I need to pee all the time.

"Take it out," Sherri demanded. "I hate those damned things."

The woman smiled again. "I've read that in a couple of your books. Your characters always hate hospitals."

"Write what you know," Sherri mumbled as she glared at the grinning nurse.

Maybe I should mention how ridiculous that scrub top is when she's working with adults. No, I'll just put it in a book.

"If your pain were between one and ten, one being the lowest and ten the highest, where would yours be?"

"About ten ccs of morphine," Sherri spat as Dylan slapped his hand over his mouth to suppress a grin behind the gaping nurse.

The woman smiled. "I'll call the doctor," she said as she turned.

"Tell him I want this damned cath out too. I can pee on my own."

"I'll mention it," she said and sped out of the room.

"You're a terrible patient," he said with a chuckle as he sat and took Sherri's hand again.

"I hate fucking hospitals." She gazed up at his handsome face. "I'm thirsty."

"I'm with you there," he said, squeezing her cold hand in his big warm one.

"What's gonna happen with Tommy?" She asked as Dylan put a straw to her lips so she could take a drink.

Dylan rolled his eyes. "That's gonna be a shit storm in Barrett."

Sherri pushed the button to raise the head of the bed into a sitting position as her head cleared. "How do you mean?"

Dylan took a deep breath. "When you weren't home by eight," he said, "I drove into town to follow you home." He squeezed her hand again. "I saw your car at The Limits and pulled in. Garret was on top of you with your skirt pulled up and was hitting you in the face with his damned fist."

"He texted me and said it was you. Said you wanted to meet for a drink."

"I know," Dylan said. "when he was telling the police you invited him, you mumbled something about proof on your phone and I found the texts." He took another deep breath. "There was something else there too."

"What?" She asked when she noted his face had turned pale. "What else?"

"The police have it now," he said, "but there were pictures of you in Garrett's arms and one of you on the hood of your car with your legs spread and his hand up your…"

"Oh, my god," Sherri gasped in horror.

"The text message with the pictures," Dylan sighed, "said they were being sent to the media, your publisher, the CW, and all the paper so they could see what a small-town slut looks like."

"Oh, my lord. Who would do a thing like that?"

"Take a wild guess," he said.

"Candi?" she hissed, "but how?"

Dylan nodded. "Garrett said it was all her idea. He had your number because of the work his company did at your house, and she told him to text, saying it was me asking you to stop for a drink. She wanted the salacious pictures and took them with her phone when Garrett grabbed you."

"What are they gonna do to her?"

"They busted her for conspiracy to assault and sexual battery, but …"

"But what?" She asked with a frown.

"As soon as they took her into custody," Dylan said with a frown darkening his handsome face, "she started screaming for a deal. She gave up her husband's meth operation and will probably get out of it with a slap on the wrist."

Sherri dropped her head back on the pillow and hissed. "It figures. Nothing changes that much in Barrett."

The nurse returned with a syringe in her hand. "Here's something for your pain," she said, "and the doctor said we can take out the cath if you're clear and responsive."

She grinned at Sherri. "I told him you were plenty responsive and seemed to be perfectly clear about what you wanted."

"Thank you," Sherri said politely, "and I'm sorry about being difficult before."

"It's certainly understandable after what happened. I can't believe Cindy … I mean Candi did that to you." She injected the needle into a port on Sherri's IV.

"She was always a bitch," she said, "and then married that no good drug dealer, but I never thought she'd do something like this." She shook her head and smiled. "I hope you ream her good in the next Hope book."

She closed the curtain around the bed. "Sorry, Dylan, this will only take a sec." The nurse folded back the blanket, reached between Sherri's legs, and pulled out the catheter. "All set," she said and picked up the plastic bag of yellow fluid to carry away.

"Thanks, Karla," Dylan said as the woman left the room.

"Karla?"

"Used to be Karla Manning, Ted Manning's little sister, but it's Karla McCord now. She married Coach McCord's son, Dan."

"Does everybody in Barrett know what happened?"

Dylan grinned. "Pretty much," he said. "Between the people at The Limit who saw it go down, the big-mouth Barrett cops, and the people working here at the hospital, word spread around town fast." He shrugged and pointed at the counter filled with floral arrangements.

Sherri suddenly felt dizzy and closed her eyes. When she woke again, the sun shone through the open blinds and she saw Dylan asleep in the chair beside the bed, covered by a thin hospital blanket.

A different nurse came in carrying a tray. "Has he been here all night?" Sherri asked the nurse.

The nurse smiled. "That man hasn't left your side since they brought you in here Friday night, honey."

Dylan lifted his head and rubbed his eyes. "What time is it?" he asked groggily.

"Seven forty-five," the graying woman said after setting the tray on the rolling bedside table and glancing at the watch on her age-spotted wrist. "You want me to bring you a tray too, honey?" she asked Dylan as he straightened himself in the chair and folded the blanket.

"No," he said, "I'm good, but I'd take a cup of that marvelous coffee you gals make at the nurse's station, though. If it wouldn't be too much trouble."

A smile brightened her wrinkled face. "You got it," she said and winked at Dylan.

"You have a way with the ladies." Sherri sipped the strong, bitter coffee from her tray.

"That's Kelly, Nigel's mom."

Sherri thought for a minute, trying to place the name. "The boy paralyzed in that car accident our freshman year?"

Dylan nodded. "She took care of him at home until he died a year or so ago of colon cancer."

"Wow," she said, "that's real dedication."

"She was a good mom," Dylan said. She got her nursing degree, took care of Nigel, and held down a full-time job."

The woman returned with a tall Styrofoam cup of coffee and handed it to Dylan. She turned to Sherri and smiled. "The doctor will be around in a bit to see you, Ms. Lambert. He knows you want to get out of here to go to that big funeral at Crider's, though I hear they've moved it to the gym at the high school because their chapel isn't big enough to fit everyone attending." She turned and scurried off.

"Sounds like it's gonna be a big do," he said and sipped the hot coffee.

"Sounds like it," she said and broke a blueberry muffin in half. "It'll make them happy." Sherri smiled and handed Dylan half of the big muffin. "I did promise you breakfast."

❧ 24 ❧

Dr. Brody released Sherri reluctantly, but knew she would leave, anyhow to attend the women's funerals. Without time to drive home and change, Sherri dressed in the black suit she'd worn to the book signing and what she'd been wearing when brought by ambulance to the hospital. She showered in the bathroom in her room and put her wet hair up in a tight bun.

"This is hopeless," she sighed as two of the younger aides on the floor helped her with makeup, using concealer to cover her black eye and swollen, bruised jaw. "I look like Frankenstein's monster."

"You look beautiful," Dylan said from behind them. He wore a tailored black suit. His mom's house in Barrett was only a mile from the hospital, so he'd driven home and changed.

"I guess this is as good as it's gonna get," she sighed. "Thanks for the help, ladies."

"We should go," Dylan said as he took hold of the wheelchair and backed her out of the bathroom.

"Don't forget to put us in your next book," one of them said. "Mandy and Cory," added the other.

Sherri smiled and said as she waved, "I won't forget. Two devastatingly beautiful ER nurses who save the lives of two handsome firemen and live happily ever after together."

"Your fans writing the books for you now?" Dylan asked with a chuckle.

"Just a little content editorial," Sherri said with a giggle.

As they rolled through the hospital lobby someone stepped in front of the wheelchair. Sherri lifted her head to stare into the glaring eyes of Laura Garrett.

Sherri's heart began to pound. The two had been bitter rivals for Tommy's affections in high school, but Laura had ended up with him.

This is not gonna be good.

"Just couldn't leave him alone, could you, Sherri?" Laura growled. "After all this time, I'd have thought you'd have given up and left us alone, but no. You invite him to that damned bar and when he doesn't give you the kinky sex you want, you hurt him and yell rape."

"I didn't ..." Dylan squeezed Sherri's shoulder to stop her.

"Have you spoken to the police, Mrs. Garrett? They have the evidence, showing that Tom is the one who texted Sherri to that bar, saying it was me."

"That's ridiculous," Laura spat and glared down at Sherri. "How would he even know her damned number if this bitch didn't give it to him?"

"I gave it to him," Dylan spat I subcontracted with him to install a heat pump in the renovation my company did on Ms. Lambert's home." He took a breath. "The business arrangement between our companies has been terminated, by the way. He took advantage of client information and used my name to commit an illegal act." Dylan brushed a finger over Sherri's swollen jaw.

"That's not true," she mumbled as tears filled her eyes. "Tommy would have told me if he was working at *her* house. He wouldn't have taken the job if he'd known it was *her place.*" Laura hissed, glowering down at Sherri. "Tommy hates her. He never wanted anything to do with her even though she threw herself at him when she knew we were going together. She even told people her and Tommy slept together when they never did. He had me he didn't need or want her."

Sherri had heard enough. "In his parents' house, in his bed, with his parents sleeping across the hall was the first time and then several other times before he married you like in the house he built for you before you were married. How do you keep that black bathtub clean? I've always wondered. It must be a bitch." Sherri watched the woman's eyes go wide. "But never after you were married. I don't sleep with married men. Do you want to know exactly where and when for the other times, Laura?"

Tears streamed down the woman's puffy face. "You're the same lying bitch you always were, Sherri. I don't know why you couldn't just leave us alone now. We have children and grandchildren, for god's sake."

"Don't put this on Sherri, Mrs. Garrett. Get the facts from the police or the DA. Talk to your husband's co-conspirator in this matter, though I seriously doubt you'd get the truth from her."

Laura jerked her head up to glare at Dylan. "What co-conspirator? What lies has this bitch been telling you?"

"Go talk to the police, Mrs. Garrett. They have the evidence and I've seen it. Your husband lured

Sherri to The Limits so Candi Clem could take pictures of him assaulting her to send to the tabloids and blackmail her out of writing another book about her high school days in Barrett. The proof is on their phones and the police have them."

"That's a damned lie and I can prove it," Laura said and rummaged in her purse for her phone. She punched the keys and then scrolled through text messages. Her face turned pale and she dropped the phone back into her purse.

"That stupid, fucking son-of-a-bitch," she snarled and marched through the group of people who'd stopped to watch the confrontation, toward the elevators.

"Uh, oh," Dylan said with a chuckle. "I think she must have cloned his phone and Tom is about to lose his other ball."

"I hope she uses a dull knife," Sherri said as she tried to calm her pounding heart.

I hate fucking confrontation. I'd rather have a root canal without anesthesia.

Dylan pushed the wheelchair toward the doors. "We'd better get a move on or we're gonna be late."

Parking around Barrett High was difficult to find. Dylan turned into the drive of The Barrett B & B where a man waved him in with a smile.

"We did the renovation on this place," Dylan said, "and I called this morning about parking here during the funeral."

"Good thinking," Sherri said with a smile. "Thanks, Dylan."

"For what?" he asked as he unbuckled his seatbelt.

"For everything," she sighed. "For saving me from Garrett, for staying with me in the hospital, and for coming with me today."

He reached across the seat and took her hand. "I'm in love with you, Sherri Lambert," he said and got out of the car.

In love with me? Did Dilly Roberts just say he is in love with me?

He opened the door and helped Sherri out of the car. She stood and was suddenly light-headed. She wobbled and Dylan caught her by the arm.

"Sit back down and I'll get the wheelchair from the trunk." He eased her back down to sit on the edge of the car seat.

I hope I can make it through this. My head is pounding, my jaw is throbbing, and Dylan Roberts just said he's in love with me. I may pass out.

Dylan brought the chair and helped Sherri transfer. He pushed her over the asphalt parking lot around the proud old Victorian painted in shades of violet and pink with white trim. It looked like a giant Sweet Sixteen cake.

"This is beautiful," Sherri said as they passed the majestic house. "You guys did a great job."

"I'd have gone with blues or greens," he scoffed, "but the owner's wife's name is Violet."

"Got ya," she said. "It's still beautiful. I'd love to see the inside some time."

He put his hand on her shoulder. "It's a date. They have Downton Abbey tea parties here, I'm told."

Sherri laughed.

"What's so funny?"

"Typical Barrett," she said. "The house is Victorian, and Downton Abbey is Edwardian."

"Oh," he said. "History ... British History, I should say, was never really my thing."

At the gym door, a man in a suit took their names and consulted a sheet of paper. "If you'll come this way, Ms. Lambert, we have seats waiting for you up front on the floor."

The bleachers in the gymnasium were full on both sides of the basketball court where rows of folding chairs were also filled with men and women in their Sunday best.

This is amazing. The women are going to be so pleased.

"Can you believe this?" Dylan asked as they followed the man to one of the front rows where he removed a chair so the wheelchair would fit. There were several flashes from cameras as they passed.

"It's certainly something," she said as she caught Louis' eye and nodded.

On the stage behind a podium sat three closed caskets. One was white trimmed in brass and the others were deep, burnished rosewood. All three gleamed in the overhead lights and had black and white photos of the women on easels in front of them.

What only Sherri could see were the glowing forms of the three young women standing behind the caskets with broad smiles on their faces.

Suddenly the gymnasium became eerily quiet and the three dead women sat around Sherri. Everyone in the room seemed to be in suspended animation, stone still with their mouths open in mid-sentence.

"Ain't this somethin,' Doll?" Molly gushed beside her. "Who are all these folks?"

"Well, that man over there with the glasses is your cousin, Louis. I believe his grandfather was with you at the Speakeasy the night you died."

Molly turned to study Louis. "He has the look of my cousin, but older. Is he smart? Louis was smart as a whip and was goin' to college."

"Very smart," Sherri said. "He and I were in

school together and he works at the Library in Barrett."

"And my kin?" Tilly asked. "Are any of them here?"

Sherri studied the faces in the front row. She pointed to a gray-headed couple she recognized from the produce market. "I think that's them over there," she said. "They own a fresh produce market here in town."

Tilly smiled and nodded. "My brother always talked about having a farm stand to sell our tomatoes, sweet corn, and apples."

Maude touched Sherri with her ghostly hand. "I know I got no kin here," she said, "but you done me proud, Doll. That casket is the prettiest I've ever seen, and my old bones are in comfort on that soft satin. It's just what I always wanted. Thank you for keeping your promise."

"You're more than welcome, Maudie and I found you a plot beside your parents and brother over in Upton."

Maude's brown eyes grew wide and brimmed with tears. "They'll like that, Doll."

"Where they plantin' me?" Tilly asked.

"In the Threewit section of Barrett Grove Cemetery, I think," Sherri said, and Molly is going to the Cummings family section."

The figures of the women grew dim as a hymn began to play and hushed voices returned to the gymnasium. A man in a suit stepped up to the podium.

"On behalf of the families of these lost women, I'd like to thank you all for coming and say welcome." He went on for another few minutes and then called for prayer. The gymnasium quieted again.

"We'll be leaving soon, Doll," Molly said in a soft voice. "I can feel it. The words are crossing us over."

"I thought that was what you wanted."

Molly grimaced. "Everybody fears what they don't know."

Sherri patted Molly's hand. "This is a good thing, Molly. You'll be back with your family."

Molly glanced at Louis and smiled. "I've missed them." She faded again.

The proceedings went on and ended with grave-side services for each woman. Sherri watched each one pass into the light hand-in-hand with lost loved ones as the final prayers were recited.

"Are you all right?" Dylan whispered when a tear slipped down her cheek as she watched Maude walk into the light with her parents and brother.

"I'm fine," she said and squeezed his hand. "I'm just glad this is all over."

"Me too," he sighed and began pushing her wheelchair toward the car. "Can you believe all this press?"

Men and women with cameras stood around the small cemetery, clicking pictures. They avoided reporters shoving microphones in their faces with questions about what connections they had to the women.

A few recognized her and asked questions, wanting to know if she felt responsible for the women because they were found in her house.

"You people are crazy," Dylan grumbled. "Those women have been dead for decades. Sherri wasn't even born then and didn't own the house. Hell," he snapped, "her parents hadn't even been born yet." He helped Sherri into the car. "You people need to get lost."

"How are you feeling?" Dylan asked as they drove back to the house.

"I'm all right," she said. "I'm just really tired."

"I'll take you home, so you can sleep in your own bed."

Sherri grinned. "And cook for you."

"Yah, that would be nice." He reached across the console and took her hand. "I meant what I said, Sherri," he said. "I love you. I've never felt like this about another woman."

"Not even Tammy?"

Dylan snorted. "It was all about lust with Tammy and then there was Carla Jean. It was never about love. We stayed together because of our daughter, but we couldn't keep it together. There was no love between us."

"I'm sorry," Sherri muttered. "I didn't mean to open old wounds."

Dylan shrugged. "Not a wound, just a mistake. I got a wonderful daughter and marvelous grandson out of it and there is plenty of love there," he said with a smile. "I'm blessed."

EPILOGUE

Sherri sat in the porch swing as she watched Dylan walking back from the strawberry patch with Kyle who clutched a basket of bright red berries in his hands. She smiled at the red smears around his mouth and smiled more when she saw the ones around her husband's.

"Look what I picked, Grandma Sherri," Kyle said as he ran up onto the porch to join her on the swing.

Sherri wiped at his mouth with her thumb. "I think you and your Paw-Paw put more in your bellies than in the basket."

"Hey, now," Dylan said with a chuckle, "we men need our strength if we're gonna catch you those catfish you want for supper."

"Don't throw 'em back just because they're not catfish," Sherri said. "I'll cook up whatever you fellas catch."

"Yah," Kyle cheered. "When can we go, Paw-Paw? Grandma and me dug a can of worms for bait this morning."

Dylan grinned down at Sherri. "She did, did she? She's a pretty good grandma."

Kyle put his head on her shoulder. "She sure is."

"Why don't you take those berries and put them in the refrigerator, and I'll fix them up later."

"With real whipped cream?" Kyle pled.

"Of course," Sherri said as the boy headed for the door.

"We're gonna have fish for supper tonight, Miles," Kyle told the big black cat that slipped out of the door when he opened it, "and I'm gonna catch 'em."

"Not if you don't get a move on and put those berries away," Dylan said to speed up his dawdling grandson.

The cat jumped onto the swing and began rubbing his big head on Sherri's breast.

"You never should have named that damned cat after *him*," Dylan snarled.

Sherri had adopted the solid black kitten after waking one afternoon to find Miles Tucker staring at her from the loveseat.

When she'd brought him home, Dylan hadn't been happy about it. He wasn't a big fan of house pets and especially not cats.

After a few glasses of wine, Sherri had broken down and told Dylan the whole story about Molly, the other women, and Miles Tucker.

A few weeks later, however, Dylan had driven her and his mother to the old city cemetery where they were met by a minister and someone from the city.

The man carried a yellowed paper rolled in his hand. "According to what I could make of this," he said and waved the paper, "Tucker's plot is over here."

He led them to a spot that had been marked with small red flags on each corner. "The city hopes you don't plan to erect a marker. It would be a beacon for crime groupies and other vandals, we fear, and would attract the wrong sort of tourists to Barrett."

Like Barrett is a huge tourist destination.

"He was never given a proper burial service?" Sherri asked as she stared down at the grass-covered plot.

"This was where the indigent, unclaimed, and unwanted were dumped by the city," he said, "None of these poor souls were given funeral services aside from being dumped in a hole and covered up."

Sherri stared across the green acreage around her and shuddered as she saw the ghostly bodies of men, women, and children—so many children begin to appear. "How many are buried here?" she asked in horror.

The man unrolled the paper and studied it. He finally shrugged. "Probably hundreds over the decades."

"Oh, my lord," she gasped, and her eyes filled with tears, "all these poor souls are trapped here and can't pass on." She slumped into Dylan, who then whispered to the minister.

"Don't worry about it, Mrs. Roberts," the minister said and patted her shoulder. "When I've performed the ceremony to send Mr. Tucker to his rest, I'll perform a general ceremony of blessing for all the other poor souls here."

"Thank you," she whispered as she stared out over the sea of ghostly figures, standing beside their burial places.

Suddenly Miles Tucker stood beside her. "What are you doing here, Doll?" he asked and swatted her behind.

"I'm sending you to the other side, Miles," she said.

"He's here?" Marilyn Roberts asked timidly from the other side of her son.

"Right here," Sherri said and pointed to the spot where Miles Tucker stood.

Marilyn stepped cautiously forward. "I hope you burn in Hell for what you did to my mother and me, Uncle Miles, and for what you did to those poor women. You were a son-of-a-bitch and I hate you." The frail, gray-headed woman turned with tears running down her powdered cheeks, stumbled back, and took her son's offered arm.

"Mary Lyn?" Miles asked, staring wide-eyed at Dylan's mother. "That's my little Mary Lyn?"

Sherri nodded. "That's Dylan's mother," Sherri whispered, "Your niece."

"Not my niece," Miles sighed softly, staring at the old woman, "my daughter."

"Oh, my lord," Sherri exhaled, and she put up her hand when Miles opened his mouth again. "I don't want to hear it."

"What?" Dylan whispered.

Sherri shook her head and smiled at the minister. "Let's get on with this and send this sorry soul wherever it is he's going."

The minister glanced from Sherri to Dylan who nodded. The man said a blessing, read a passage from the Bible and then asked them all to bow their heads in prayer.

Sherri watched Miles as he began to fade. It surprised her when Molly, Tilly, and Maude appeared.

"Hey, Doll," Molly said cheerfully and waved with a large iron padlock in her petite hand. "We're here to see Miles to his eternal rest." For some reason, it didn't surprise Sherri to see the women being followed by small, dark apparitions carrying an iron cage that might hold the man if he was sitting with his knees bunched up beneath his chin uncomfortably.

That would be a hell of a way to spend eternity and if anybody deserves an end like that, it's Miles Tucker.

The minister then did a blessing of the entire cemetery and soon, all the lonely souls were led away into the light by waiting family or friends. Most were led away happily. A few, however, like Miles, went away followed by dark, unforgiving spirits with cages.

Those poor souls may wish the minister had never come to release them from this plain of existence.

Sherri sat with the cat while she waited for Kyle and Dylan to return from Barrett Lake. Their life had been good, and Sherri couldn't complain.

Thomas Garrett, with the testimony of Candi Clem, had been found guilty on all charges and sentenced to twenty years to life in the state prison. He'd appealed his conviction and lost. Tom had been shanked one night and found dead in his cell the following morning.

Candi had made a deal to testify against her husband and he too had been sentenced to twenty years in prison—the same prison as Tom Garrett. Candi had gone into the witness protection program and taken her mother with her when she left Barrett for places unknown.

Sherri's follow-up book to Lost Hope, Hopeless, told the story of the characters in Hope, Colorado, forty years after high school and how their lives had changed—or remained the same. The book became a bestseller and the CW optioned it for a future made for television movie or series.

Karla Jean remarried, and her new husband wanted to move to Alaska and live off-grid with his new bride—only his new bride. Kyle came to live with his Paw-Paw Dylan and Grandma Sherri, though his grandparents in Mississippi hadn't been happy about it.

Dylan bought his brother out of Realistic Renovations with the help of a silent partner. Bobby moved to Las Vegas with the money he received. Sherri took over the office duties and helped with stylistic details of the renovations. She also took control of the advertising and built on Bobby's Holiday ideas. The company had expanded and had successful divisions in three states.

Life was good and Sherri could only see it getting better.

Dear reader,

We hope you enjoyed reading *Dreams of Molly*. Please take a moment to leave a review, even if it's a short one. Your opinion is important to us.

Discover more books by Lori Beasley Bradley at

https://www.nextchapter.pub/authors/lori-beasley-bradley

Want to know when one of our books is free or discounted? Join the newsletter at

http://eepurl.com/bqqB3H

Best regards,

Lori Beasley Bradley and the Next Chapter Team

ACKNOWLEDGMENTS

I'd first like to thank my readers. I wouldn't be here without you.

Thank you to Mrs. Sally Taylor, my Senior English teacher at Benton Consolidated High School who told me never to forget the story I wrote about a dream I had where a girl was buried in the floor of an old house. She said it would make a great book someday. It's taken forty years, Mrs. Taylor, but here it is. I hope you're not too disappointed. Thank you for seeing something in me that few, including myself, did.

While I'm back at BCHS, I'd also like to thank Mr. Lou Ceci. I think you saw something too. Thanks for all your encouragement over the years.

Thanks to my group at The Central Phoenix Writers' Workshop. You read a few of the first chapters of this and as always helped me sort through the kinks.

To Tiffany Rock who read my first draft of this novel and pointed out some serious continuity issues. This is the fourth draft. Thank you.

As always, please leave a review—good or bad. I can't fix my mistakes if I don't know what they are.

Dreams Of Molly
ISBN: 978-4-86750-007-1
Mass Market

Published by
Next Chapter
1-60-20 Minami-Otsuka
170-0005 Toshima-Ku, Tokyo
+818035793528

3rd June 2021